THE CON GAME

by

Michael Cronin

Dales Large Print Books
Long Preston, North Yorkshire,
BD23 4ND, England.

British Library Cataloguing in Publication Data.

Cronin, Michael
    The con game.

    A catalogue record of this book is
    available from the British Library

    ISBN   978-1-84262-799-0 pbk

First published in Great Britain
in 1972 by Robert Hale & Company

Copyright © Michael Cronin 1972

Cover illustration © Valentino Sani by arrangement with
Arcangel Images

The moral right of the author has been asserted

Published in Large Print 2010 by arrangement with
Watson, Little Ltd.

Dales Large Print is an imprint of Library Magna Books Ltd.

Printed and bound in Great Britain by
T.J. (International) Ltd., Cornwall, PL28 8RW

PROLOGUE

A man escaped from Greece with the police close behind him, much too close for safety. George Missounis had serious charges against him, and although he reached Italy he knew he had little time to spare if he wished to preserve his liberty.

Yet he expected all would be well when he joined up with Peter Pastranou, because Pastranou was the veteran Master Mind in these matters, and subversive action against the current regime in Greece was meat and drink to Peter Pastranou.

All did indeed go well. They were resting in a small country house outside Genoa; there was to be a boat to take them away – but it was not yet ready.

One early morning, three police cars arrived. But they were not early enough and they made too much noise breaking in: eight Italian policemen, and two Greek agents as fellow-travellers.

An ambitious Inspector led the way up the stairs and burst into the room, with a

7

revolver. He was too quick and entirely too ambitious. Before he could lift his arm, Pastranou broke it and took the revolver from him.

Using the Inspector as a shield, he pushed him to the top of the stairs, and those below dared not shoot. He then tossed the Inspector down amidst the posse, and sprayed them with revolver shots. Two he killed, three he gravely damaged. So there was a scuttling for cover below.

Pastranou and Missounis left by a rear window and ran through the garden to where the Volvo waited. Those of the police who had recovered themselves began to shoot from the hedge. Missounis fell against the car. Pastranou pushed him in and drove off.

Missounis had a bullet through his leg just below the knee. He was bleeding heavily. But there was no stopping yet for first-aid.

Pastranou had a nose for country roads. Genoa would be shut to them, and the airports. Pastranou drove north. He had no choice.

The first time Missounis fainted and fell against him, Pastranou was angry. Then he found time to stop and do what he could about the bleeding. George Missounis was largely unconscious now.

In the early stages of their escape Pastranou twice changed cars, arranging the transfer with considerable aplomb even when he had to carry Missounis. First he took a Fiat parked by a coppice while the driver attended to a call of nature. The Fiat had a full tank, and the Volvo was left immobilised.

Then came a Citroen. A honeymoon car with the brand new luggage in the rear. The bride and the groom were occupied elsewhere in the shade.

Missounis needed medical attention badly now. In a remote hillside village Pastranou found an elderly doctor and gave him enough money to jerk him into action, and without too many questions, a bullet wound being undeniably a bullet wound. And as soon as they were out of sight, the septuagenarian doctor would be on the telephone.

So Pastranou changed direction, joined the main road heading up to Torino for a few miles, and then swung east, and into the mountains again.

George Missounis was now unfit for further travel. They needed a place where he could hide and rest, and this was a good country for hiding. Mountains and deep

9

empty valleys.

Pastranou had a number of undercover contacts around the Mediterranean. Daniele was the man for the present emergency. He would know of a place, and he was reliable if the money was right.

By nightfall Pastranou had located Daniele, and they had agreed on terms, steep terms because this was no frolic and George Missounis was in a bad way. He would not be walking for some weeks. He would need sheltering and feeding and guarding. And the police were after him. Which pushed Daniele's price up.

To cover the expenses and meet Daniele's bonus would take more than Pastranou carried with him. Also it was easier to hide one than two, so it was agreed that Pastranou would get himself back to London and raise the money, more money. Daniele would send reports of the patient's progress to Pastranou, and by the time Missounis was well enough to be moved the search would have cooled, probably.

Pastranou would devise some suitable way of getting Missounis out of the country, and the semi-conscious Missounis was now in no fit state to consider the pros and cons. They carried him in the dark up a slope to a hut where Daniele said he would be safe for some days at least.

Pastranou gave Daniele all the money he could spare, and set out on his journey back. The search was on for him as well, especially for him. One of the men he had wounded was now dead, so the score against him was three. If they caught Pastranou they would catch George Missounis.

It took Pastranou four days to reach Marseilles by devious means, and three days later he was in London.

PART ONE

1

Sam Harris was a little surprised to find himself chatting up this bird one afternoon in a tea shop, because it is widely known that he spends the minimum of time in such establishments, especially when they are run by well-bred ladies with pearls and Kensington voices.

This was one of those extra-expensive Surrey dormitories, much favoured by highly rewarded entertainers, managing directors, and other such solid citizens, where few of the publicised properties would change hands at less than forty thousand – snug homesteads with their three-car garages, swimming pools, tennis courts, and landscaped gardens.

The 'Avalon' fronted the village green, and it had all the right trimmings: leaded windows, black and white timbering, home-made chow, copper warming pans on the walls, cosy little tables. Not Sam's scene.

But Sam's car had broken down, the petrol pump had gone on the blink, and he'd been forced to walk a sweaty mile and a half to a garage, which was not his favourite exercise. So now he had to put in the time while he waited for the car to be fixed. It was too early for the pub across the green, which left the tea shop.

He took the only vacant seat, at a table with a girl. She wasn't a bird because she was wearing large glasses and she was reading a book. A teacher, or some kind of student, he reckoned. Brainy. So who needed a brainy girl with glasses. Sam had never heard of Dorothy Parker, but they thought alike.

When he excused himself like a little gent as he sat down she gave him a bit of a look and nodded and went on reading. She could please herself, Sam wasn't bothered. A duchess arrived and Sam ordered – assorted sandwiches, a pot of tea and cakes.

He was the only male in the place, apart from a small boy in a blazer eating a large pink ice. There were plenty of middle-aged biddies who had never been short of a bob or two. No crisps, cokes or juke boxes. Too much glass for any of that. Like being in a church, as far as Sam could remember.

The chow arrived, and Sam dug in. Squirting little sandwiches damn nearly

16

transparent, and a tiny chunk of walnut cake covered in goo. The tea had hardly the strength to trickle out of the spout.

All the same, Sam was feeling pretty good and lively, because it hadn't been a bad trip, in spite of the car. His ex-wife was about to get hitched again, she had found herself another mug, a bloke who ran a pub near Farnham, and not a bad pub at that. Ethel had been working there in the bar for a few months already, and Sam was sure she hadn't been sleeping alone.

What had cheered Sam was the thought that she wouldn't be on his back for alimony, not that he had been paying it all that regularly, only when the conniving cow had caught up with him, and that hadn't been too often, Sam being a gent who kept on the move for a number of other reasons as well.

When the girl shut her book and took off her glasses she looked a heap better; her eyes were large and brown, and nothing like as snooty as he had thought. Not a bad frontage either under that sweater.

She was about to leave, she fumbled with her bag, and it slipped to the floor. Like a greyhound out of a trap, Sam was down getting it for her, which gave him a good view of her legs under the table. Terrific. A real surprise. So he didn't hurry and she knew he was looking at them, she even smiled. She didn't twitch her legs about. Smooth tights all the way up there.

Sam straightened up and gave her the bag.

'Thank you,' she said, 'that was clumsy of me.'

'Not at all,' said Sam. 'My pleasure.' And he thought she knew what he meant. 'Very nice,' he added, and he didn't mean the Avalon.

She was looking very amused, which wasn't a bad start. She was ready to leave, but she was still there. Sam never needed a kick in the ribs to move on from a good opening with a bird, and she was definitely now a bird. With legs like those she couldn't be anything else.

'Excuse me,' he said, 'But you must be in show business. Correct me if I'm wrong, but I've seen you somewhere, on the telly, wasn't it?'

That got a nice laugh out of her, and some of the tea-sipping biddies stopped their yakking and stared at them.

'I'm sorry,' she said. 'It must have been somebody else.'

'I could have sworn,' said Sam, giving her

some of the old sincere stuff. 'I mean, you've got the looks, if I may say so.'

She laughed again, not so loud this time. She wasn't insulted. You never insult a bird when you tell her she looks like some glamorous bit. It gets them thinking – maybe you're right, then you're half way home. That was Sam's experience. Ladle it on thick.

'You'd photograph beautifully,' he said. 'No kidding, I know.'

'I just work round here,' she said. 'Don't tell me you're a producer or something else exciting, because I don't think I'll believe you.'

Sam grinned, his candid small boy grin. 'I'm in business. I just happened to be passing through. I'm glad my car broke down or I wouldn't be here – you don't mind if I say that? It's the truth.'

'You must be joking,' she said. 'Nothing interesting ever happens here, but nothing.'

'We could do something about that, you and me.'

'Now I know you're joking,' she said. 'I don't even know your name.'

'Sam Harris,' he said, and immediately wondered why he hadn't used one of his bird-bashing aliases. His footwork must be slowing up.

'I'm Ellen Scott,' she said.

'That's a good name, Ellen,' he said. 'Sort of dignified.'

'Dull and homely you mean,' she said.

'You couldn't be more wrong,' he told her.

They went on from there, on the good old pattern of the casual pick-up, and Sam spread himself, coaxing plenty of laughs out of her. It passed the time, and the more he looked at her the prettier she became. So why pass up a possibility? And she wasn't slapping his face.

They left together, and several pairs of eyes watched them. A pick-up at the Avalon. How frightfully common. That girl from those awful Dobells, wasn't it? What could one expect? And that dreadfully vulgar little man with the crinkly ginger hair. Probably a commercial traveller and we all know what they are.

Ellen walked with him to the garage. She was nearly as tall as he was, but kind of graceful with it, and those long legs moving out of that mini skirt had Sam fascinated. Trying not to watch them too obviously was making him nearly cross-eyed.

His car was ready, a new pump had been

fitted. He had been hoping to pay by cheque, but the garage manager wasn't amenable and Ellen was there listening to them, so he had to pay cash, which was something he avoided doing whenever possible – nobody who knew Sam ever willingly accepted one of his cheques.

'Well you're all right then,' said Ellen.

'Give you a lift?' he said.

'I don't live far away,' she said. 'It really wouldn't be worth taking you out of your way–'

'Why walk?' He opened the passenger's door. This was the bit when she ought to walk away. She got in beside him and settled those fabulous legs of hers comfortably. Easy. She wasn't much more than twenty or so. Fresh.

Sam hadn't picked up a bird as young as that for a very long time. Most young birds who came his way always found excuses when he put it to them. Sharp little cows. This was new territory, and only an easy hour's run down from London.

Under her directions they had driven round the green; in the middle there was a bit of grass with ropes around it, and she told him that was where the cricket team played and they had some pretty famous players as well, county players. Big deal, thought Sam. Also there was a golf course of some repute, but it was expensive and hard to get into unless you knew somebody and had the right background.

Sam was no cricketer and no golfer, but he encouraged her to prattle along with her travelogue. When he had to change gear he gave her some of the hand treatment high up on her thigh, and she wasn't screaming then either. Made-to-measure. Easy.

They were on a private road. High walls and hedges. Fancy gates and somebody had been sweating over those grass verges. If she lived along here her family had to be loaded, and Sam's imagination began to churn over at the lovely possibilities. All the really rich birds he had ever known you could stick in your eye and they wouldn't make you blink.

So maybe this might be it. Rich birds sometimes married ordinary blokes, and Sam had never honestly thought of himself as ordinary. He had the touch, the little bit extra that made all the difference. All he needed was the right opening. Then he knew he would move. Boy how he would move.

Latching onto a bird who lived in one of these places? That took brains, and Sam had them. He knew.

When she told him to stop by some ornamental gates he was determined he wasn't going to let it end there. *Langley House* was worked in gold paint into the ironwork of the gates, and he could see part of the house inside at the end of the drive. Thirty rooms maybe. Awnings. Flowerbeds. Lawns. All the right stuff for easy living.

'You live there?' he said.

'Sort of,' she said. 'That's where I work.'

'Work?' said Sam, staring at her, disappointed. 'What sort of work?'

She was smiling. 'You seem surprised … now just what do you think I do?'

'Search me,' said Sam. A bird who worked for her living, like anybody else.

She put her hand on his leg and squeezed, laughing at him. 'Oh, Sam, if you could see your face. Are you terribly disappointed that I'm just another working girl?'

'Not a bit of it,' he said gallantly.

'I work for the Dobells,' she said. 'That's their house up there. I help Mrs Dobell, sort of secretary.'

'Must be a pretty nice job,' he said.

'It is, they're nice people to work for, especially Mrs Dobell. You've heard of Mark

23

Dobell, haven't you? He's very wealthy, almost a millionaire.'

'I don't come across many millionaires, to tell you the truth,' said Sam.

'You'd like him,' she said, which Sam found flattering, as though his approval mattered. 'You'd never think he had all that money, and he made it himself.'

'Good for him,' said Sam. 'I don't suppose you get much time to yourself?'

'I get all I want, usually,' she said. 'Mrs Dobell does a lot of work for charity, she's on committees ... and they entertain a lot, so I'm kept fairly busy most days.'

'Wouldn't suit most girls I know,' said Sam, 'not living in on the job, I mean–'

'Oh but I don't actually live in the house,' she said. 'There's a gardener's cottage Mrs Dobell had done up for me, I'm really quite private. Unless there's work to do I can come and go just as I please.'

'Sounds okay,' said Sam.

'It is,' she said. 'It's the best job I've ever heard of. There's a private entrance across the garden, and I have a key to the gate. I can usually borrow a car if I ask in time and they aren't needed, and I can eat with the family if I feel like it.'

She smiled at him. 'I'm not exactly a

servant, Sam.'

'I didn't think you were. I think you must be a smart girl to hold down a job like that.'

A bird in the country with her own pad might be worth knowing. It would make a sweet change from the lousy bed-sitters that came his way, with some old bitch of a land-lady creeping about and listening for the bedsprings.

'Well,' said Ellen, 'it's been nice meeting you, Sam, and thanks for the lift.' She was about to get out and that would never do.

He held her arm. 'Wait a minute,' he said, 'you don't have to rush—'

A car's hooter blared commandingly behind them, and a scarlet Porsche, the snappy 911S model, drew alongside and braked dramatically. The driver had blonde hair tied up in a spotted scarf; she wore enormous wrap-round dark glasses, and a pale blue sleeveless sweater.

'I say,' she called out, with the Porsche angled across the front of Sam's BMC Eleven Hundred – not yet paid for by any means nor ever likely to be '–you're rather blocking the entrance—'

When she saw who was sitting with Sam a quick smile flipped across her face, making her look young and not as arrogant as she sounded. 'Sorry, Ellen, I didn't see it was you–'

She lifted one hand in farewell, the Porsche took off and swept into the drive, throwing gravel, exhaust snarling.

'That's Kitty Dobell,' said Ellen, 'the daughter of the house. She's a bit wild, but I like her, we get on all right.'

'Nice car,' said Sam.

The Porsche had come to a skidding halt in front of the house. In flared blue trousers, Kitty had bounced herself out. She undid her scarf and she was taking a long look down the drive. Sam had the impression that she might be smiling. Now there was a dolly bird all right. And with money.

'If you like cars,' said Ellen, 'you ought to see Mr Dobell's Rolls, it's beautiful.'

'I'd settle for the Porsche if I could afford it,' said Sam. 'When am I going to see you again? Make it soon.'

'You mean you really want to?' She wasn't being coy, just serious.

'I'm asking you,' said Sam. 'Right? This is my lucky day, like I told you.'

She chewed her lower lip, amused. 'I think you're married, Sam.'

'Was once, not now,' he said. 'As a matter of fact, I've just been hearing about my ex, she's getting married again, so I'm laughing. We could pop up West, have a meal, do a show, anything you fancy. How does that grab you?'

'I think you could be a dangerous proposition, Sam,' she said.

He lifted both hands to show how innocent he was. 'They don't come more harmless,' he said. 'We'll have ourselves a ball, right?'

She was examining him, still slightly amused at his speed. 'We might do that,' she said.

'When?'

'Tomorrow evening,' she said. 'I have to see Mrs Dobell off from Paddington. She's going to Bristol and long car journeys make her ill. If I find I don't have to go with her, I'll be at the hotel, will that do? About seven?'

'Fine,' said Sam. 'I'll look for you.'

'If I have to travel with her I'll leave a message at the desk.'

'I got my fingers crossed,' said Sam.

She got out of the car and walked briskly up the drive, and she didn't look back. Presently she heard Sam drive away. Kitty had left the driver's door of the Porsche open, which didn't have to mean she expected to be driving again, simply that she assumed somebody would shut the door for her. When she finished with anything she just dropped it and moved along. Clothes, or men, it made little difference to Kitty.

Ellen went up the wide stairs to a room on the first floor that Mrs Dobell used as her home office. There was some routine correspondence to attend to. Ellen put on her glasses and sat at her desk; through the open window came the busy pop-popping of a lawn-mower, and the pleasant summer scent of flowers and cut grass. As she typed she thought of that odd little man, Sam Harris. So eager and sure of himself. Saucy. And Sam Harris wouldn't have liked the way she was smiling.

A little later the door opened and Kitty came in. She didn't knock: it wouldn't ever cross her mind that she wasn't instantly welcome, and it wasn't only because she was the daughter of the man who paid Ellen's salary. The two girls were friends.

Kitty perched on the arm of a chair. 'Was that your new boy friend, Ellen?'

'Just somebody I met.' Ellen went on typing.

'Interesting?'

'I don't know. I only met him this afternoon.'

28

'I get it,' said Kitty. 'Where did you pick him up? You've only been in the village, and I know he isn't a local.'

'We had tea at the Avalon, if you really must know.'

Kitty rolled herself into the chair, laughing.

'How quaint. I didn't think it could happen like that any more. A pick-up in a tea shop!'

Highly entertained, Kitty stretched; she wore no bra and she was a well-developed girl. Ellen allowed herself to smile without stopping her work.

'It was the best I could do,' she said.

'Are you going to see him again? Or isn't it any of my business?'

'Maybe,' said Ellen.

'Now that's a smart answer,' said Kitty, unabashed. 'Score one to you. What's his name?'

'Sam Harris, that's what he told me.'

'He wasn't fooling you,' said Kitty. 'Nobody would make up a name like that, and he looked just like Sam Harris ought to look, if you follow me.'

Ellen whipped the paper out of typewriter. It was faultless, as ever. 'Don't insult my friends,' she said. 'It's not the mark of a lady.'

'Get out,' said Kitty indulgently. 'No ladies here, only us girls. What does this chap do?'

'I really don't know,' said Ellen. 'I didn't ask him.'

Kitty shook her head in mock reproof. 'You surprise me, letting yourself get picked up like that.'

'No lasting harm done,' said Ellen, tidying the letters in the tray ready for Mrs Dobell's signature.

She knew there was no sure way of getting Kitty to shut up when she was in one of her we're-both-girls-together moods, allied against the rest of the stodgy household. Kitty had recently returned from an exclusive Swiss finishing establishment where the strict rules had been even more strictly enforced, where the regulation social and cultural visits had been so closely supervised that there had been no chance for a young lady to get herself chatted up by any unsavoury male. It had been one of the very few places where no nonsense was taken from the spoilt offspring of the super-rich.

So Kitty was now making up for lost time. She had enrolled at an expensive School of Art in the West End, mainly as a giggle and because it gave her an excuse for keeping odd hours with even odder company. And

Mamma Dobell was too busy with her good works to know what was going on.

Blue-eyed, authentically blonde, almost twenty-one, Kitty was ready for anything, but anything.

Ellen knew. More than once she had provided Kitty with a handy alibi, and she knew how active and varied Kitty's sex-life was.

'He's too old for you,' said Kitty, speaking as an expert.

Ellen gave her a bland smile. 'Nice of you to show such interest, but you're all wrong.'

Eventually, bored at the lack of response, Kitty took herself off. Ellen waited for a while, then went along and listened outside Kitty's door. She could hear the shower going. Kitty always took a shower when she was bored. And Mrs Dobell was out of the house. Good.

Back in the office Ellen dialled a London number, she spoke quickly and quietly. 'Joe, it's Ellen – I've just met somebody, I've got an idea … he looks a bit like George, I think … no, just another man, he hasn't a clue – please listen, Joe – I'm meeting him at the Station Hotel at Paddington tomorrow night. I'll be in the upstairs lounge after seven … no, of course he doesn't know a thing – he thinks he picked me up, and I want you to see him…'

Joe was laughing.

'Please be there,' she said. 'I'm not being silly, Joe.'

Highly amused, Joe said okay, he'd look in. Did she want him to tell old man Pastranou?

'No,' she said. 'Not until you've seen him, and we've had time to talk.'

'You're a crazy girl,' said Joe. 'See you.'

Sam Harris had a piece of pie and a light ale in a pub in Notting Hill. The bar wasn't too full yet. Lucky Lane slid up to him, shoving his half-empty glass along. He was a small and unimpressive character, who wore a raincoat irrespective of the weather. A grafter. Known as 'Lucky' because nine years back he had nicked a packet from a bookie in his own house – the bookie's house.

It had been near Richmond Park, in the middle of the afternoon; the bookie had been engaged upstairs with a bird who just happened to be an acquaintance of Lucky's, and Lucky had nipped over the back wall, as quiet as a cat. He had left by the front door with close on two thousand quid stuffed here and there. In broad daylight.

The luckiest tickle of the century, never to be repeated. Since then Lucky had been in and out of jail. Petty larcenies. No class about them at all, but he would still bore the pants off you if you gave him half a chance. An incurable optimist. Full of wind.

'Sam,' he said in a sort of whisper, 'I got summink good–'

'Beat it,' said Sam, sourly. 'I'm not interested.'

'This is a real red-hot proposition,' said Lucky with much earnestness. 'Honest, Sam.'

'So mind you don't go and get yourself scorched.' Sam shifted along the bar, to indicate that the conversation was over.

Lucky inched along after him, darting a cautious look all around. It was a real pantomime to watch Lucky on the job. He'd been run in by the fuzz so often that he looked for disaster round every corner, and frequently he wasn't disappointed.

'Won't cost you nothink to lissen,' he said.

'You're bad news,' said Sam. 'It does me no good even to be seen with you. So go and chew somebody else's ear. I'm not interested.'

Lucky wagged his head at the obtuseness

of some people.

'You're passing up a real good thing,' he said. 'I need a partner, so I thought of you, Sam, that's fair enough, right?'

'What is it this time?' said Sam. 'You knocking off the Bank of England? Do me a favour, Lucky...'

'Lissen,' whispered Lucky. 'There's this greengrocer's shop over in Wembley–'

'With your kind of luck that would be Henry Cooper's shop,' said Sam. 'You've heard of Henry Cooper, the heavyweight champion?'

'Think I'm daft?' said Lucky.

Sam finished his drink. 'You took the words out of my mouth. Find another mug. I'm busy.'

Lucky muttered something about toffee-nosed bastards, and he didn't mean the heavyweight champion. Sam patted him on the back to show that there were no hard feelings, and left.

Sam's current location was a semi-basement, semi-furnished apartment; it was cheap and it was convenient, and the fact that the neighbourhood had an unsavoury reputation bothered Sam not at all. The nightly alarms and excursions he took in his stride, if he happened to be at home, which was not always.

The premises on the floor above were periodically used for the production of blue flics, and Sam's own place had been sublet, unknown to the landlord, from an ageing lady who'd had the good fortune to find an elderly gent to pay her summer overheads in Majorca.

It was Sam's intention to move out before the lady returned from the sun-drenched beaches, in which case she could whistle for the balance of her rent. He gave a little thought to Ellen Scott and *Langley House,* and the blonde Kitty with that red Porsche.

Now there was a contact that should be worth something, if he handled it right. It was never a waste of time to mix with the people with real money – some of it just might rub off.

That was a comforting thought. You could scratch about for years, getting a crust here and there. Then– Boom! There was the opening right in front of you. So grab it, boy.

2

Joe Feeny was in the late twenties; dark, not particularly handsome, of medium height, in a business suit of conservative cut, not trendy, just right for a rising young executive in one of the better firms – oil, property development. Tucked under his arm was a thin black leather case.

He was browsing at the bookstall by the left luggage office when he saw Ellen coming. She had seen the Bristol train off, getting rid of that fussy old bag, Mrs Doris Dobell.

They had the stall to themselves. Ellen went through the business of looking over the magazines, moving closer to Joe.

'See what you think of him,' she said quietly. 'I think he might be all right.'

Joe nodded. 'Don't rush him. I'll be around.'

When Ellen went into the hotel Joe was just a few yards behind her, and he was paying no attention to Ellen's very graceful rear view and elegant movement, because he knew how she looked and how she moved without clothes, and he had other things on his mind.

Sam was there at a table by the main stairs so that he had all the entrances under control. He had already checked at the reception desk and there was no message for him. Attractive birds frequently left Sam dangling at the last minute, but not this time, he was happy to note. She wore a mini-skirted outfit in lime green, and he thought she looked even better than he had remembered.

'I'm not late, am I?' she said.

'Bang on time,' said Sam, taking her arm to steer her across the perils of the lobby. 'How about a little drink to start with?'

'Lovely,' she said, as though he had suggested something quite original.

Joe followed them into the bar and took a stool near the table Sam had selected. The bar was fairly empty, and Joe intended to hear most of what was said – not that he didn't trust Ellen's judgement, she could do this kind of thing better than most women, but a lot depended on it.

She was drinking vodka, and it took a lot of that to get her off balance. Joe unzipped his case and began to frown over pages of type, sipping his whisky and nibbling salted peanuts, and listening. Before long he thought he had Sam Harris pegged: a fiddler, and not a very successful one either. Shifty. He'd think a couple of hundred quid was a fortune. Probably had a police record.

Ellen was doing a good job, flashing those legs just enough to have Harris on the twitch and wondering when he could get at her. Simple technique, and it almost never failed. Sam Harris was being conned by an expert right out of his class.

Sam thought he was putting on a pretty good act himself, and he had her laughing and full of the joys of the old boy-meets-girl routine. She wasn't asking him any awkward questions either, such as what he did for a living and where he lived, and so forth. A very promising opening all round.

'Where would you like to eat?' said Sam.

'I'm in your hands,' she said and smiled at him to show they were both thinking of the same thing.'

'Wish you were,' said Sam.

'I see I'll have to watch out for you,' she said very happily, her brown eyes warm and full of life. 'You might be more than a girl like me could cope with, Sam. I mean, we're practically strangers, aren't we?'

The notion of Ellen playing hard to get had Joe Feeny almost choking over a peanut, but Ellen knew exactly what she was doing.

Sam smiled the potential winner's smile. 'Plenty of time to get acquainted,' he said, 'and I wouldn't call us strangers. Let's drive down to Soho and try one of those French or Italian places, and you don't have to worry about the last train back because I'll drive you. Okay?'

'That would have been nice,' she said, 'but I have a car up here. I drove Mrs Dobell, our local train service isn't too special.'

That rather put a kink in Sam's plan to drive her back and see what might develop on the way and when they got there – mostly when they got there.

'I'm sorry, Sam,' she said. 'I didn't have much choice. The next time I'll come up by train.'

He patted her hand on the table. So there was going to be a next time. 'You do that,' he said masterfully. 'One for the swing of the door, and then we eat, right?'

'I know quite a pleasant restaurant near here,' said Ellen. 'You can get a table on the balcony and the park is right there opposite.

We could walk it from here.'

'Anything you say, I believe I know the place,' said Sam expansively. He had been past it many a time but the pub further down had the kind of prices he was used to. However, this was an investment.

Joe followed them out and down towards the park: Sam's bouncy confident figure alongside Ellen's elegance. Big deal for Sam. Joe watched them enter the restaurant and presently appear on the balcony under the pretty coloured lights.

Some two hours later Sam was seeing Ellen into the black Mercedes 220, the family runabout, parked near the station, and when Sam drove out into the Bayswater Road towards Notting Hill Joe was close behind him in a Mini Utility.

He saw Sam get out and dart down into the basement of a tired old building, and he knew he hadn't been wrong about Sam's resources – if this was home for Sam Harris he certainly wasn't in the money, which should make it easier to swing. Joe drew up a little further along and waited, to make sure. Sam might just be visiting his aged mother. Or calling on a tart. There was activity going on in the neighbourhood – music and voices, coloured voices mostly.

After a while a coffee-coloured girl detached herself from a nearby doorway and drifted over. She wore a green pyjama suit and carried a miniature white poodle.

'Lookin' for some action, mister?' she suggested, leaning over him so that he smelt her and the dog as well.

'Just waiting for a friend,' he said.

The girl told him something not polite and went back to her doorway. When a tall thin coloured lad appeared beside her and then began to move across the pavement, Joe Feeny started the car and drove off. He had things to do and getting sliced wasn't one of them.

Ellen was waiting for him at his flat. She had her own key. She had kicked off her shoes, and she was quite at home there.

'What do you think?' she asked eagerly. 'It isn't all that crazy, is it, Joe?'

He heaved her out of her chair, adroitly weaving his arms about her so that her feet left the floor. Then he held her in a kiss in mid-air before putting her down, and her face was flushed in a way that perhaps Kitty Dobell might have envied.

'You're a clever kid,' said Joe. 'I've been

thinking about it and it might even work – shave off that moustache and he just might be George.'

'I wonder how we could put it to him,' she said.

Joe Feeny gave her a knowing smile. 'After what I saw tonight that shouldn't be too difficult; he was drooling over you – not that I could blame the poor mug. You set him up and we use him.'

'I wish I could think of a better way of doing it,' she said. 'It'll be dirty.'

'It's a dirty situation,' said Joe. He ran his hand up and down her back. 'You don't have to take it too far, sweetie. Just diddle him along … we'll give it plenty of thought.'

'Could we make him a cash offer?' she asked.

'We couldn't trust him,' said Feeny. 'You know his type, and old Pastranou would never agree to do it that way… I think your original idea has possibilities, if you think you could carry it through. It's saucy enough to work … come to think of it, you're a pretty saucy little thing yourself–'

'No, Joe,' she said, 'there isn't time–'

'There's always time,' he said, leading her into the one bedroom.

This had started three weeks ago between

them, and it was still at the instantaneous combustion stage, certainly for Ellen. The very sight of him was enough to weaken her, no matter who was there. It was like a drug, and she couldn't have enough of it once he touched her.

How deep it went for Joe, beyond the simple physical attraction, she couldn't tell, but he was a skilled lover and made her feel momentarily that there was nobody in the world but the two of them.

Perhaps she wouldn't have let it happen if she hadn't been so worried about George, and if Joe hadn't been part of Peter Pastranou's outfit. She had never quite understood how Joe had come in with Pastranou, because Joe didn't share Pastranou's political interest, or George's for that matter. Joe was Irish, and something of a drifter … a natural-born rebel, he said. And unattached. Also it was clear that Pastranou trusted Joe, and Pastranou didn't trust many people.

It was as wonderful as ever, but quick. It would never do to have Pastranou suspecting there was something between her and Joe, and they were able to meet like this only in Joe's flat. And she knew that when this business with George was done she wasn't likely to see much more of Joe. They both knew there could be nothing permanent in this, which perhaps made it all the sweeter, for her.

'You'd better go on ahead,' said Joe while she was doing her face. 'Give old Peter the rough outline, then I'll arrive and back you up. We'll chew it over, all three of us.'

They were waiting for him at the Hammersmith flat, Pastranou's place. Pastranou was about fifty but looked older, which was deceptive because he had the toughness and resilience of a fit man half his age. He had a brown face and little hair, and small hard blue eyes. Stocky, rugged, he could still swim five miles, scale an unclimbable cliff, and strangle an armed guard with silent efficiency – if necessary, and without feeling he had done anything worth shouting about; he had been close to sudden and violent death so often that now he had small regard for human life, including his own, which made him a bad man to provoke.

As far as personal records went, he was apparently unmarried, but he had contrived the parenthood of a number of children, mostly female, which was a secret sorrow.

He ran a lucrative antique business near

the Broadway, and was something of an authority on icons which were having a vogue, here and on the other side of the Atlantic. He had also more than a passing interest in Renaissance miniatures, and when he talked about Eastern ceramics the curators of well-endowed museums were likely to listen attentively.

A man of many parts and many faces. And much sought after in some areas.

'Ellen has been telling me something about this nobody you have found,' he said.

'He's a nobody all right,' said Joe Feeny. 'A drifter. I've seen where he lives.'

'So you think he would suit us?' said Pastranou.

Feeny glanced at Ellen. 'He'd be easy, wouldn't he?'

'No trouble,' said Ellen. 'Do I have to sleep with him?'

She had been sitting alone on a settee. Now Pastranou came over, sat beside her, and patted her thigh, one of his very rare gestures of affection. She might have been his daughter, almost. 'Would that be too unpleasant for you, my dear?'

'If I'm going to see much of him he'll expect it,' she said.

'So,' said Pastranou, smiling, 'you will

45

make the sacrifice, and we will all be most grateful.' He squeezed her thigh encouragingly. 'You are a beautiful girl, you will be wasted on this nobody, but it is necessary. Now it is important for us to find out how much he might be missed, and only you can do that safely. We must have more background details, particularly who might come asking about him.'

'People do disappear, even in this country,' said Feeny. 'We could make him one of them.'

'Find out for sure,' said Pastranou.

'We know he's pretty broke,' said Feeny. 'He's on the dodge. Don't you think so, Ellen?'

'He's a big talker,' she said. 'There's nothing behind it, just wind. But he fits otherwise; he's the right build and the right height. I don't think his nerve is very good.'

'A small-time opportunist,' said Pastranou thoughtfully. 'I begin to like it very well.'

'He's a natural,' said Feeny. 'I've seen him and I agree with Ellen.'

'No wife,' said Ellen. 'He says he's divorced, and I think that's the truth. He hasn't mentioned any other family. I didn't push him too hard, not the first time out – he isn't all that stupid.'

'Just stupid enough.' Pastranou smiled. 'I must see him before we go any further.'

'The day after tomorrow,' said Ellen. 'This is going to be a regular courtship. I'm coming up by train, so he can have the fun of driving me back afterwards.'

'You've got him hooked all right,' said Feeny.

Ellen shrugged. 'He's also very interested in the Dobells; all that money sort of had him mesmerised, and then we saw Kitty Dobell in her sports car and his mouth watered. I fancy he likes knocking about with a girl who mingles with the rich. Gives him some kind of a kick – he'd be thrilled if he knew that Kitty was asking me about him.'

'That could confuse the issue,' said Pastranou. 'You must keep him away from her. You should be enough for a man like that, more than enough.'

'Leave him to me,' said Ellen. 'I'll have him borrowing money from me before long, I shouldn't wonder. I'll get him to take me to *Bianchi's*, Peter, then you can have a look at him.'

'A lamb to the slaughter,' said Feeny.

'Shut that up,' said Pastranou flatly. 'It is necessary. Now, Ellen, you know what we need to know about him, a picture as complete as possible, and you know what time we have left to us.'

'Ten days,' said Ellen. 'Then the Dobells are off to the States for a month or so, and Mrs Dobell has finally made up her tiny mind that she won't be needing me with them after all; the boss will have a brace of his own staff to run the errands.'

'And the villa?' said Pastranou. 'That will be available?'

'She made the offer very graciously,' said Ellen, 'and I of course accepted just as a little bonus.'

Feeny grinned. 'Very sweet all round.'

'I have my uses,' said Ellen.

'You are a good girl,' said Pastranou. 'Without you we could do nothing.'

Ellen stood up. 'I'll have to be going. What's the word from the other side?'

'It is still difficult,' said Pastranou, 'but it will be all right.'

'You mean there is no news,' she said. 'How is he?'

'His leg is healing and he walks better each day – the little walking he is able to do. I think he is getting impatient to move on now. That is understandable, for a man of his temperament, but I will get word to him

48

that he must be patient a little longer.'

'Give him my love,' said Ellen.

Peter Pastranou nodded, walking her over to the door, one arm around her shoulders. 'They will never take him again, be sure of that.'

'Keep on letting me hear you say that – I get frightened when I think of how close to him they have been,' she said.

Pastranou tapped himself on the chest. 'I have had them that close to me many times – here I walk about London as free as the air. I have a good business, I make enough money, I am a respectable citizen. And I have friends where I need them. Last week there was a judge of the High Court taking sherry with me in my parlour over the shop, after I had sold him a bargain; the Commissioner for Police is a client of mine, and there are many others of excellent reputation. Do you think I would risk all that if I were not sure of myself and what I do?'

Joe Feeny yawned, but it was behind Pastranou's back, which was wise of Feeny because Peter Pastranou was touchy about his heroic exploits.

'Have no fear for George Missounis,' said Pastranou. 'He is a young man after my own heart. Even if he is half English.'

Ellen smiled. It was an old joke, without hurt. George was her step-brother, some five years older.

'Don't blame me,' she said at the doorway. 'We don't choose our parents, Peter – even you didn't do that; you just happen to be a Greek.'

'I could be nothing else,' he said. 'At least your mother had the good sense to marry with a good Greek first. Nikolas Missounis was a patriot, and he died a patriot's death–'

'With a bullet through his chest,' said Ellen quietly. 'My father caught pneumonia, Peter. He died in his bed, quite unheroically. No dramatic gestures. He just died.'

'I know,' said Pastranou. 'It was very sad for your mother. He was a good quiet man.'

'He was all that,' she said. 'He never understood George. They agreed on almost nothing.'

'It was not to be expected,' said Pastranou. 'And it was no discredit to either – an English accountant and the son of Nikolas Missounis, even after being educated at one of your English schools – they were of different moulds. Now I would be happy to have George as a son of mine, so I am doing all I can to see those pigs do not get their hands on him again. This is my kind of affair, it makes me young once more: being so respectable so long makes me uncomfortable.'

She was smiling as she went down to the car. It was impossible to be in Pastranou's company for long without feeling some of her natural optimism return.

It was nearly two o'clock when she put the Mercedes in the garage; the maroon Rolls was there, so Mark Dobell was at home, and the scarlet Porsche had been parked at Kitty's usual untidy angle. She felt the radiator. It was still more than warm. There was a light in the sitting-room of her cottage.

Kitty was waiting for her, sprawling on the chesterfield that was just too big for the tiny room. Her blue eyes were bright and sharp, and Ellen knew the sweet sickly smoke in the room.

'I wish you wouldn't smoke that stuff in here,' she said. 'I've asked you before, Kitty. Your parents would play hell if they knew.'

'A little pot never hurt anybody,' said Kitty lazily. 'You really should get yourself turned on some time. You don't know what you're missing.'

'No thanks. Now if you don't mind I'd like to get to bed.'

'Have fun?' said Kitty.

'Dinner,' said Ellen, 'after I saw your mother off.'

'Until this hour?' said Kitty, smiling. 'That must have been quite a meal.'

'We talked.'

'I bet.'

Ellen opened the windows to air the room. She noticed that the picture of George had been moved from where she kept it on the table. Kitty was often trying to get her to talk about George, the step-brother who looked so unlike her. Kitty would like to think there was some illicit romance there – she didn't really believe the brother and sister bit.

'You look frustrated, duckie,' said Kitty. 'Didn't he measure up then?'

'I'm going to bed,' said Ellen. 'Good night, Kitty.'

'Wouldn't you like to know what kind of evening I've had?' Kitty sat up, hugging herself, shaking the loose blonde hair away from her face. A fallen angel.

'You went to a party and you met another fab man,' said Ellen. 'Right?'

'Correct,' said Kitty. 'He was an Indian, a Hindu. He said he was a Swami, but he wasn't a bit holy.'

'I can imagine,' said Ellen.

'I've never seen a man with such hands,' said Kitty dreamily. 'Absolutely wicked, if you know what I mean.'

She shook herself, slid inelegantly off the chesterfield and picked up the shoes she had kicked off. Ellen collected the ashtray Kitty had been using, with the squashed pale stub that still held the give-away odour.

'If the police came here,' she said, 'we'd both be in trouble.'

Kitty giggled. 'The fuzz.'

'They watch out for reefer parties,' said Ellen. 'They probably know all about the mob you were with tonight. You really ought to ease up a bit, Kitty, before you're in serious trouble.'

'And you know what's wrong with you, little mousie,' said Kitty, 'you're too scared to live, you'd stay awake all night if you drove through a traffic light.'

Carrying her shoes, she padded uncertainly to the door, bumped against it, and turned round, looking suddenly pale and sick. She dropped her shoes and closed her eyes.

'Think I must be a little bit smashed,' she murmured.

Ellen knew the drill. She took her into the

53

bathroom and held her head while she was sick. A very young sad Kitty now. She cleaned her up. And Kitty was weeping a little. Mostly about that Swami who definitely hadn't been a holy man. Kitty would listen now, but it would all be gone by tomorrow. She would go her own way.

Ellen made her drink some coffee and walked her across to the house and in through one of the many side doors, whispered a good-night, and went back to the cottage where the stale smell of the reefer hung in the pretty curtains.

'Little mousie', Kitty had called her. Afraid of her own shadow. Just before she fell asleep she was thinking of Sam Harris, and what was ahead of him, and it would not have pleased Sam if he had known.

3

Peter Pastranou was there at the little bar when Ellen came in with Sam, and when they eventually moved in to eat he had the next table, and Sam throughout remained unaware of his presence. He was just another middle-aged bloke who had to dine alone, whereas Sam Harris was right in there pitching – with the only dolly bird in the place hanging on his every word. Sir Oracle in full flood.

When Pastranou got up to leave he gave Ellen the faintest nod, which told her all she needed to know.

'A passport?' said Sam. 'I can get one – are we going somewhere?'

'I've had the offer of a villa near San Remo,' said Ellen. 'Rent free ... would you be interested?'

Sam wagged his head, smiling as the thought began to come over him. 'You mean you and me? What's the catch?'

'Does there have to be a catch?' said Ellen. 'I just thought you might like a holiday in the sun. It's a lovely spot, the Dobells own the villa and they're going to be in America, so Mrs Dobell suggested I might use it. I'm due for a holiday, and it wouldn't be all that much fun on my own.'

'I bet you wouldn't be on your own for long,' said Sam warmly. 'I've heard about those blokes over there.'

'I might need protection.' Ellen's smile was full of meaning. 'I don't really care for those Mediterranean types. But of course, if you've made other arrangements, Sam, I'd quite understand.'

'It isn't that,' said Sam. 'You mean this is a straight invitation?'

'Why not,' she said. 'If you didn't think you'd be bored, away from your friends and all that.'

'Friends!' said Sam disgustedly. 'Listen, Ellen, if I emigrated tomorrow nobody would shed a tear. A lot of ghouls, that's what they are, and that goes for my ex-wife as well.'

'You think about it,' said Ellen. 'It really wouldn't have to cost much. I'm taking a car and there'll be loads of food at the villa.'

'I've thought about it,' said Sam. 'I just can't believe you're serious.'

'I'd feel safe with you,' she said demurely.

Sam reached across the table and patted her hand. 'We'll talk about it on the way home. I told you it was my lucky day when I met you in that tea shop.'

Before he left her that night by the side gate – she didn't invite him in and he didn't press the matter – he had promised to shave off his moustache: she had a very sensitive skin and it might give her a rash, she murmured into the side of his neck, especially when they'd been sun-bathing in that lovely Mediterranean sunshine. His mind flooded with erotic possibilities, Sam was in the mood to promise her anything: he would undertake to shave his skull to the bone if it made her any happier!

Ellen giggled. 'Just the moustache,' she said, 'and do it before you have your passport picture taken.'

'It comes off first thing in the morning,' said Sam.

'You're sweet,' she said. 'Have you ever been abroad before, Sam?'

'The Isle of Wight,' said Sam, grinning.

'I think you'll like it,' she said. 'I was there at Easter with the family and we had a marvellous time. There's just one thing, Sam – I'd rather you didn't tell anybody else. Not that there's any reason why we shouldn't take a trip together, we're both adults and all that, but people do talk.'

'Not a word,' said Sam.

'The Dobells won't mind,' she said, 'because you're a friend of mine, so that will be all right.'

Sam nodded, delighted. 'This is private, you and me. Anyway, I don't have to explain to anybody where I go or what I do.'

'You don't think I'm being silly?' she said.

'Nothing silly about it, the way I see it. To hell with all of them, it's our business.'

Her smile was a little uncertain. Sam pulled her back into his arms and embarked on another necking session, and found her willing enough. Afterwards he watched her go in by the side gate, and before she disappeared into the bushes she waved at him, schoolgirl stuff but very nice for all that. He drove back up to London in a continued state of exhilaration. It was falling right into his lap. Better and easier than he had ever hoped for.

The semi-basement apartment looked really tatty when he let himself in, and he would have to make very sure that Ellen never found out where he lived. A villa on the Mediterranean, and for free, with his own bird thrown in: Sam knew half a dozen young stallions with bedroom records who would jump at the chance ... and they would never believe that Sam Harris was the boy who had snaffled it.

In the morning he shaved off the sandy moustache; it had been carefully tended in the past, and now it was off without a qualm. It made him look younger, he thought, and he wondered why he hadn't done it before. It was a pity he didn't strip better: no chest to speak of and skinny legs. He'd have to get by with some snappy Continental slacks and shirts, Italian gear.

Ellen was going to be extra busy for the next few days, with the family pushing off to the States, so they wouldn't be meeting for a week. But they would make up for that, too bloody true they would.

Popping into his local for a quick light ale that morning he ran into a neighbour, Sophie Randall, a middle-aged scrubber with whom he'd had a couple of quickies soon after he'd moved into the district. Not an old bag yet but pretty near and not getting any better.

He had to fend her off, but she was still hung-over from last night and beyond the reach of any insult he could think up.

'What you been up to, Sammie boy?' she wanted to know. 'Didn't know you when you come in, straight – I thought it must be your kid brother ... you don't half look different without your whiskers–'

She created such a song and dance that everybody in the boozer knew, which decided him that it was going to be smarter to keep away from his usual spots. He'd have a nice quiet week and save his strength for later.

Joe Feeny travelled tourist class to Paris and then on to Nice. He was just another holiday-maker in search of the sun and without too much spare cash to throw around. He wore stout walking shoes and carried his gear in a rucksack. A pleasant open-air type of young man, not too talkative, but obviously respectable. His passport described him as a clerk, and he attracted no kind of attention.

He was checked through the Customs at Nice, and there was no trouble. He was manifestly not the kind of traveller to carry a small automatic under his left arm, snug in the armpit so that it didn't impede his movements. Having been cleared at Nice he was passed through at *Ponte San Luigi* without any further check, on the speedy SATI Autolinee bus into Ventimiglia over the border.

The bus was crowded, which suited Feeny. He had been over the route before, and the beautiful coastal scenery of the *Riviera dei Fiori* – the Flowers Coast – meant little to him. What was more important was the fact that the bus was up to time, and a little over two hours after crossing the frontier he was in his modest room in the old quarter in Porto Maurizio.

He behaved like any other tourist of limited means, exploring the old town on foot, but carefully avoiding any contact with the other English visitors, and speaking to few people, although his Italian was more than adequate. He sent Peter Pastranou a highly-coloured postcard of the palatial modern *Prefettura* building, with some police cars in view. The simple message he sent was 'Wish you were here' which would amuse Pastranou, perhaps.

Later on the following afternoon he was sitting at a table outside an open air café on the *Piazza Savona* in Alassio, just in front of the railway station. Drinking a modest glass of *bianco*, watching the passing scene and waiting, in the bland sunshine.

When Daniele arrived he made no sign and he didn't sit at the table. In his faded blue working trousers and open-necked shirt, he shambled past, looking sad and preoccupied, perhaps not quite sober; a rough roly-poly lump of a working man.

Feeny got up and followed him, under the archway and into the *Via Adelasia*. There was a small dirty van parked by the pavement. Daniele got behind the wheel but he didn't start the engine. He gave a nod as Feeny walked past with his rucksack strapped on his back, and Feeny was a mile along the road and out into the beginning of the hilly country before the van drew up, to offer the hitch-hiker a lift.

'In the back,' said Daniele.

Feeny climbed in among the sacks and cartons, unslung his rucksack.

'You got an English cigarette, old cock?' said Daniele. 'You remembered to bring me some?'

Feeny passed a packet forward. Daniele had worked in Soho for some years as a waiter, and he had acquired a ripe Cockney accent, along with a taste for English cigarettes and draught beer. He had also done rather better than average with the English girls, according to his reminiscences and in spite of his quite unromantic appearance. He had a refreshing directness of approach – bam-bam … very nice, duckie.

He drove the elderly van with a great deal of style and verve; like most of his compatriots he became highly competitive as soon as he got behind a wheel, and the gear box screamed as he did his racing changes.

Joe Feeny was having an uncomfortable

ride, but he knew it was no good appealing to Daniele to ease off. Every minute they spent on the road they were wide open to a police check, and every time Daniele slowed Feeny tensed himself and waited – hitch-hiking tourists seldom found their way so high in the mountains, and if they stopped the van it would be a toss-up whether they got away with it or not.

The country police would be courteous enough, but they weren't peasants, and Feeny couldn't afford to spend any time in a *Commissariato Di Publico Sicurezza*, in a police post in any of the small hill towns, satisfying police officials that he was a bona fide tourist who happened to like travelling the mountains on foot and at night. Daniele was a local and his cover was foolproof.

It was dark by the time Feeny was allowed to sit up in front with Daniele. They had been climbing for over three hours now, and the dark uneven hills were all around them; the road snaked around, with low stone verges and long frightening dark abysses dropping into nothingness.

They were meeting very little traffic, which was a good sign; emphatically this was no road for a novice, or for any vehicles without good brakes and steering. Daniele was no novice, and the van was better than it sounded.

'Any action recently?' said Feeny.

'Too bleeding much,' said Daniele.

'Serious?'

'They got Piero two nights back.'

'He won't talk, will he?' Feeny couldn't keep the uneasiness out of his voice.

Daniele glanced at him. 'Maybe not. They missed his woman…'

'Well, that's better then,' said Feeny. 'It could be worse. How did they get him?'

'We knew they had been watching that road from Pinerolo down to Saluzzo,' said Daniele. 'Three times I made the trip myself, always at night … so they know me, mister, and they pass me through; I am okay, see. They search a little maybe, but there is nothing – always I make the funny joke about my hot baby waiting for me.' He eased his paunch under his belt. 'They stopped Piero in Ravello, and they find his gun before he can throw it away, so Piero runs – and they run faster… I am always telling him about that goddom gun, but he don't listen.'

There was a pause, then Daniele went on: 'You got a gun, mister?'

'Yes,' said Feeny, 'you know damn well I have.'

A hitch-hiking tourist with a little automatic tucked snugly under his left armpit, he would arouse interest.

'If they stop us, I don't know you,' said Daniele. 'I just give you a lift up into the mountains. We lost two men now in three weeks … it is fouling up, mister.'

'Not too healthy,' Feeny agreed, and wished that Peter Pastranou had come as well. This was his kind of thing. Hide-and-seek in the mountains, with the police blocking all reasonable exits, and there was no way of getting information back to Pastranou, not with safety: a trunk call to London from some village inn would probably be listened to, and Pastranou would blow his top.

Feeny loosened his slacks, and undid the money belt around his middle. He took out some notes, folded them and stuck them into Daniele's side pocket. 'Get them to Piero's girl,' he said. 'Where are they holding him?'

'Saluzzo,' said Daniele. 'They got him good and tight.'

'We'll just have to hope that he keeps his mouth shut. Get his girl right out of the district; we can't have her hanging around in Saluzzo. She could make trouble – can you fix that?' said Feeny.

'I fix,' said Daniele.

'You know Piero,' said Feeny. 'Do you think he'll talk?'

'That depends on plenty things,' said Daniele. 'Piero he comes from Catanzaro, mister, and respectable people in these parts reckon nothing but bandits ever came out of Calabria, so they may push Piero around a little and have a big laugh at the stupid peasant with his gun in his belt, who don't know yet how civilised people are living here in Piedmont.' Daniele himself was a native of Turin. 'They got no record of him here, he just another ignorant peasant ... so maybe he spend two-three weeks in a cell while they push him around, then perhaps they kick him out – bloody nice all round, hey?'

'It would be,' said Feeny.

'Piero bloody dumb when he feel like it,' said Daniele. 'Got a little police record in Palermo, mister. I know that for sure.'

'How little?' said Feeny.

Daniele grinned and made quick slicing motions with the side of his hand. Chop-chop.

'So we'll have to hope they don't search that far,' said Feeny. 'Can you let him know we're looking after his girl? That might

66

make him feel better.'

'I see,' said Daniele. 'Maybe day after tomorrow they let me visit.'

'They mustn't connect him with us,' said Feeny.

'Mister,' said Daniele, 'police are the same everywhere, suspicious bastards. It's the way they think, okay? They give Piero a hard time just for the hell of it. Sonsabitches.'

'Too right,' said Feeny. 'Every last one of them. You haven't told me how our friend George is making out. All under control with his end?'

Daniele puffed out his plump cheeks, shrugging, a real piece of pantomime. 'Glad to be seeing you – when that old Pastranou coming?'

'Soon, early next week. We've been working out something new; it'll be all right.'

'It better be,' said Daniele. 'We running short of money, mister – you got some?'

'Would I be here otherwise?' said Feeny.

They swept round a tight curve under an overhang of rock and trees where their exhaust boomed dramatically, and Daniele braked harshly at the sight of the slowly swinging light ahead.

A policeman straddled a motor cycle and blocked the road, waving them down to the side, and they could see the lights of other vehicles further up. Feeny had been waiting for something like this, but now that it was happening he didn't feel all that confident in Daniele's ability to talk them through.

With growing relief he listened to the rapid exchanges between Daniele and the patrolman, and his Italian was good enough for him to hear that there had been an accident on the next bend – a car had driven over the edge, breaking through the wall and tumbling down into the scrub. Three people dead at least. The road was still open but they were to proceed with extra caution...

Daniele made the appropriate noises of sympathy, and heartily agreed with the officer that some people should never be allowed behind the wheel of a car. He offered his assistance, like a good citizen, and was told that it was all being taken care of.

They edged carefully past the scene of the accident. There was a police car there and one other civilian vehicle, and a knot of spectators. They saw the gap where the wall had crumbled, and the men with ropes lowered over the edge. There was a lot of waving of hands and torches, but not at their discreet passing. There was sudden death down below in the broken wreckage of a car.

They passed the other policeman who was positioned to warn traffic coming in the other direction, and Daniele gave him a comradely salute.

Later he said, 'They got there bloody quick, mister. I never met a police car up on this road before, not at night. We better find ourselves another road before we run out of luck – we don't want to meet no more coppers.'

'We don't,' said Feeny. 'Is there another road?'

'Long way round,' said Daniele.

Some miles along he turned off; there was no signpost; just a dusty track, wide enough for the van; it was rugged travelling, with a loose rutted surface and plenty of blind bends, and dark hills frowning all around them. The van was smelling hot, and Daniele nursed it along. Several times he stopped and switched off and let the engine cool, while they stood by the wayside and smoked Feeny's cigarettes. Now and then there was a glimpse of a distant yellow light from some isolated cottage perched on the hillside. They met no traffic at all. This was sheep and goat country.

It was almost ten o'clock when they reached a junction, left the track and moved on to a slightly better road. Rounding a corner their light lit up the pleasant sparkle of water falling down the hill.

'*Colle di Fontans,*' said Daniele. 'Very beautiful waterfall, mister. Soon we come to the village, San Bartolomeo.'

'I hope it's got a pub,' said Feeny, shifting wearily on his seat.

'Very nice pub,' said Daniele. 'We eat there okay. Maddalena is expecting us.'

'Maddalena?'

'Real smart girl,' said Daniele. 'She work there; her uncle Lorenzo owns the pub, but Maddalena runs it – she is the sister of Anna, Piero's Anna.'

'Safe?' said Feeny. 'How much does she know?'

'She mind her own business,' said Daniele.

There were too many odd women mixed up in this end of it, Feeny was thinking. But he said nothing.

San Bartolomeo was larger than he had expected. There was a cobbled square, a large church, and plenty of lights still in the buildings; a few people still about. The pub

70

was on the edge of the village, and there were some cars parked in front of it.

Daniele ran the van into a side alley by the pub where there was a farmyard of sorts, with a gate and outbuildings. They went through the yard, and it smelt of manure and chicken droppings and pigs, and entered the pub by the back door, and it was clear that this was Daniele's normal method of entry – he had picked his way across the littered yard with no fuss.

They were in a large low kitchen, stone-floored, with a massive wooden table, a tall dresser loaded with china, a modern electric stove, and an old-fashioned stone sink. The old open fireplace was still there, with a high over-mantel and baskets of cut logs ready for the winter. There was a beautiful smell of food. From the front rooms of the pub they could hear the rumbling voices of the customers.

'I get Maddalena,' said Daniele. 'We stop the night here, okay?'

The idea was attractive to Feeny. 'How much further have we got?'

'Two, maybe three hours ... not good walking at night for you.'

Feeny sank into a high-backed wooden chair. 'Let's eat first and think about it,' he

71

said. 'I don't fancy hill-climbing in the dark.'

'We make an early start in the morning,' said Daniele. 'Be quicker that way–'

'And maybe I won't break a leg,' said Feeny. 'I'm no goat. Will we be all right here?'

'Nobody gotta know we're here,' said Daniele. 'Only Maddalena.' He went out for a few minutes and when he came back the girl was with him. Maddalena.

4

She was a tall girl, dark and slender, with an intelligent face and smooth healthy skin. Not beautiful but distinctly attractive, in a white blouse and a short dark skirt. She was the kind of girl who would know what she was about, well able to keep importunate males in their place. Easy moving and competent.

Speaking English, Daniele introduced Feeny as his friend from England.

Maddalena smiled as she said, also in English: 'You are very welcome. We do not see many visitors from your country.'

'When I get back I'll spread the news abroad,' said Feeny.

'You are hungry,' said Maddalena, and forthwith busied herself with the stove. Men were always hungry. 'I make you *Cotoletta alla Milanesi* – you like veal cutlets in egg, Mister Feeny? With melted cheese and tomato?' And without waiting for him to answer she went on with her preparations. Very brisk and businesslike. Anything she cooked was bound to be good, and very soon the kitchen was filled with an appetising smell. She set two places on the table, and produced two mugs of *espresso*.

There were two rooms they could use for the night. Quiet rooms. She would see to them while they were having supper. She asked no questions. Watching her move about her kitchen, Feeny wondered if she had a lover. He thought she would be good in bed – dark passionate, made for loving. But what kind of a life could she be leading up here in the mountains? Working all hours?

He caught Daniele's eye. Daniele shook his head as though guessing what he had been thinking.

'I take a little look around,' said Daniele.

73

He went out.

'Is business good?' said Feeny, feeling he had to say something.

'We make a living,' said Maddalena. 'It is mostly quiet. There is little here to attract the tourists.'

When Daniele came back in he was disturbed. 'Mister,' he said quickly, 'time for us to be going – there is somebody out there who should not see us.'

'Trouble?' said Feeny.

Maddalena stared at Daniele. 'There has been a stranger here, before tonight as well, I have noticed him, but he talks very little … always he watches…'

'A little man,' said Daniele, 'in a dark suit?'

Maddalena nodded. 'I do not know his name. He speaks Italian, but he is not one of us.'

'Greek,' said Daniele. 'Demetriades, one of those. Secret Police, mister – no good to us.'

'He would not come in here,' said Maddalena. 'You have time for your supper–'

'Did he see you?' said Feeny.

Daniele shrugged. 'He is a smart bastard. I was not expecting to see him out there. I think he is by himself.'

74

'There has never been anybody with him before,' said Maddalena. 'I should have warned you. I guessed he was somebody from the police–'

'We're leaving,' said Feeny. 'There'll be no trouble for you, Maddalena. I'm sorry about the supper.'

She smiled. She still stood at the stove. The door into the yard opened very quietly. The man who stood there was small. He wore a dark suit with the jacket buttoned high, a stiff white collar and a narrow tie. With his sloping shoulders and neat small shoes, he looked like a middle-aged clerical worker, except for the gun he held.

Slowly he advanced into the room, glanced briefly and warningly at Daniele, then looked at Feeny.

'English,' he said, 'I speak English.'

'That's nice,' said Feeny. 'Who are you and what makes you think you need that gun?'

Daniele began to smile, and Maddalena was frozen into immobility by the stove. Feeny was sitting, both hands on the table in front of him, and he was nearest to the intruder. If only he had been standing he might have tried something with his own gun. This must be Demetriades, and

Daniele said he was a smart bastard.

'Your name?' said Demetriades. 'What are you called?'

'You have no authority here,' said Feeny, 'I don't have to answer any of your questions. If you have any standing with the Italian police just show me your credentials, and in the meantime you can put that damned gun away.'

Demetriades circled the end of the table, kicking a chair out of his way. His sallow face with the too-heavy moustache showed he was getting angry, perhaps because there was a young and attractive woman present.

'You,' he said to Daniele, 'on the floor … over there.'

Daniele squatted, and was told to put his hands on top of his head. Demetriades looked at Maddalena.

'No,' she said placidly, 'I have my cooking, I will not have good food wasted – it is *Cotoletta alla Milanesi* and it would spoil. Perhaps you would like some when you have done with your business? There will be plenty.' She appeared quite undisturbed.

'Signora–'

'Signorina, *per favore*,' said Maddalena, turned her back on Demetriades, and attended to her cooking.

'You could shoot her,' said Feeny reasonably. 'She isn't looking, you'd be safe.'

Moving with unexpected speed, Demetriades slashed his gun against the back of Feeny's head, bouncing his face down on the table. Then he grabbed Feeny by the hair and forced his head back and rammed the gun under Feeny's right ear.

'Fonny joke,' he said in a fierce whisper, bending close over him.

'You've got halitosis,' said Feeny. 'You ought to change your diet, get more exercise.' He was trying to slide his right hand into his armpit without making too much of a business of it; his eyes were streaming from the smack against the table. He was hoping Daniele wouldn't do anything rash – that gun was digging into him, and it was just possible that Demetriades would use it.

'What do you do here?' said Demetriades.

'On holiday,' said Feeny.

'So you come in here by the back door, and you prepare to eat your meal out here in the kitchen.'

'We're shy,' said Feeny. The fingers of his right hand were now almost touching the holster, but he couldn't go any further without risking having his head blown off.

Demetriades solved the problem. He yanked Feeny backwards, dragging the chair with him, over to the unyielding stone floor. Caught unawares, Feeny was momentarily stunned; his jacket flew open. Demetriades stamped on his wrist and stooped quickly and took the gun from its holster, then he stepped back, a gun in each hand.

Daniele had been crawling forward beside the table. Now he halted.

'We will see who has the bad breath now,' said Demetriades.

He gestured with both guns at Feeny. 'Get up, English comedian, and answer what I ask. Get up now.'

Slowly Feeny sat up. His eyes were clearing, although his head still rang with the bump on the floor. His line of vision took in the trousered legs of Demetriades with the shiny shoes, and the smooth brown legs of Maddalena with the sensible sandals by the stove.

He saw Demetriades lift one foot to kick him in the back, and he tilted his head just in time to see Maddalena swing the loaded pan off the stove and fling its contents into Demetriades' face.

Demetriades gave a high-pitched squeal, dropped his guns, and covered his face with both hands, scalded by the hot fat, stagger-ing.

Feeny grabbed Demetriades around the knees, brought him down, and crawled up his body to get his hands on his throat, and everything he touched was slippery with hot food. But he got a grip and pressed hard, while Demetriades bucked and wriggled under him and tried to claw his face.

Daniele had picked up both guns. 'Get him quiet!' he whispered. 'Quick!'

Shoving with both hands against Demetri-ades' throat, Feeny began banging his head against the floor, up and down, viciously, on and on, until he was feeling no more resistance. He stood up and looked at Maddalena.

She was still shaking, one hand over her mouth, the dripping pan still hanging from her other hand – appalled at what she had done, perhaps.

'That was neat,' he said.

'No,' she whispered. 'Now there will be trouble...'

Customers were calling for her from the front of the inn. She put the empty pan back on the stove, looked down at the mess on the floor, and Demetriades.

'He is dead?'

79

Daniele was kneeling by Demetriades. 'Not dead,' he said quickly. 'We will get him out of here, I promise–'

'The police,' she said, 'they will come–'

Daniele led her over to the door. 'See to them out there,' he said. 'It will be okay … let nobody come in here yet. We will take him away. Nobody will know.'

'He has the German car,' she said. 'It is the only one.'

'Remember,' said Daniele, 'you know nothing – if they come here asking about him, you know nothing – he left the inn, and you have not seen him since … go now and serve their drinks. Later come back and clean the floor.'

She went out without another word. They carried Demetriades across the room to the back door. His face was mottled, shiny.

'Smells better than he looks,' said Daniele. 'You hungry, mister?'

'Not now,' said Feeny. 'Get his keys.'

'Skinny little bastard.' Daniele rummaged and found two lots of keys, he took both. 'Bloody near killed him.'

They put out the light and opened the back door and waited a moment, Demetriades hanging limply between them. 'Okay,' whispered Daniele, 'into the van.'

Demetriades was stirring by the time they shoved him among the sacks; he was making unhappy sounds.

'I'll stay with him,' said Feeny. 'Got any rope?'

'Under the seat,' said Daniele, moving off into the darkness.

Feeny found a coil of rope under the passenger's seat, and very soon Demetriades was tied hand and foot and he was conscious enough to start protesting until Feeny hit him smartly on the side of his jaw and promised him plenty more if he didn't act sensibly. The only awkward moment came when a solitary man came round from the front of the inn and paused to relieve himself against the wall a few yards from the back of the van. Feeny had one hand on Demetriades' mouth and the other just as hard on his windpipe. There was no disturbance. The man wandered past, whistling. And Feeny allowed Demetriades to breathe again.

It seemed a long time before Daniele arrived with the car, but it was only a few minutes. The car was a black Volkswagen, and he left the engine running.

'I take the van,' he said. 'You follow – you got him fixed good?'

'Good enough,' said Feeny. 'What are we going to do with him?'

Daniele pulled Demetriades up, found a sack and tugged it over his head, and shoved him back. Then he locked the back of the van. 'We talk later,' he said.

Feeny got into the Volkswagen, and he knew they couldn't afford Demetriades as a passenger where they were going. He thought of Maddalena – there was nothing wrong with her nerve. She had put herself in serious danger on their behalf … how soon would Demetriades be missed? And then what? He thought he knew what Daniele had in mind.

They were doing some laborious driving, over poor roads, and Daniele was being very careful, stopping occasionally and evidently looking for somewhere. There were no sign posts. Nothing but the loose surface of a country road with scrub and dark hills and murderous corners.

After some forty minutes of tortuous travelling, the van stopped. Daniele got out and walked to the edge of the track where the hillside dropped away. He stood looking for a moment, his hands in his pockets.

Feeny joined him. Daniele made a rolling-over motion with one hand and smiled.

'There could be a bad accident here,' he said. 'Bloody bad road, hey?'

Feeny got the picture. And he thought of all the arguments against...

'If we take him with us,' he said.

'How?' said Daniele abruptly. 'We have to do this, mister. He is a Greek policeman – that is enough, okay?'

'He's still alive,' said Feeny.

'You ask George Missounis when we see him,' said Daniele. 'You ask him if we do right. Demetriades would shoot both of us if we give him the chance – he is from the Greek Secret Police, mister.'

Daniele walked quickly back to the van, unlocked the back and got inside. Feeny waited, then went over. What Daniele said made sense. It had to be done.

Daniele had cut the rope. He had propped Demetriades against the side of the van, and from the way Demetriades drooped it was clear that he wasn't conscious.

'Drive the car up by the edge,' said Daniele. 'I fix this bastard ... we give him one bloody good push.'

Feeny drove the Volkswagen to within a yard or so of the edge of the track, the engine running and in neutral. They carried

Demetriades over and put him behind the wheel; his head fell over it, and Daniele jammed him in hard spreading his arms so that he wouldn't fall away.

He wiped Demetriades' gun and put it in his pocket, along with the second lot of keys.

'You push, mister,' he said. 'You push bloody hard.'

Feeny got behind and shoved. Daniele had let the hand-brake off, the Volkswagen started to roll.

It went very quickly and quietly, then it began to hit something below and the rear lights went up and over. There was a harsh clanging and a sound of rending metal, far below, and a whoosh of flame and smoke rising.

Daniele nodded briefly at Feeny, and they went back to the van.

'You don't look so good, mister,' said Daniele.

'How long before they find him?' said Feeny.

'Long time, maybe,' said Daniele, and started to drive.

'He'd have to report in somewhere,' said Feeny. 'He wasn't just floating around on his own; somebody will be expecting him to turn in a report.'

'So they look for him,' said Daniele. 'Maybe they don't find him.'

'He got too near,' said Feeny. 'Maddalena said he'd been there before, and that's too near for comfort … there'll be more of them visiting San Bartolomeo when they don't hear from him.'

'They won't hear anything,' said Daniele. 'We don't talk to coppers much … nobody's gonna admit they even saw the Greek – we just a lot of dumb peasants, we don't know nothing.'

'I'd like to know just what brought him to the village,' said Feeny.

'Coppers nose about,' said Daniele. 'It don't mean they know anything for sure. The last time I saw Demetriades he was at Vercelli, pretty close to fifty miles the other side of Turin–'

'Which makes it all the more worrying that he was at San Bartolomeo tonight. It's too damn close.'

'Didn't do him much good,' said Daniele.

'My gun,' said Feeny. 'I'd like it back.'

Daniele dug in his pocket and handed the little gun over. 'Didn't notice you waving that around much at the pub, mister – you shoot good?'

85

'You must try me sometime,' said Feeny pleasantly enough.

Daniele turned the van off the track and they bounced along among some trees, very slowly; a better vehicle with lower ground clearance would never have made it. Daniele parked the van under some bushes that made a screen almost to the ground, and they got out.

They had been climbing, they were high up, it was coming up to midnight, and the air was distinctly chilly, but in his open-necked shirt and thin trousers Daniele didn't seem aware of it. He waited while Feeny slung his rucksack over his shoulders.

'Now we walk,' he said. 'And we don't use no bloody light, so you watch where you put your feet and you be okay, mister.'

And with that he struck off through the wood with a very purposeful air; if there was any kind of a path Joe Feeny couldn't see it; it was dark under the trees, and some of the trees had roots that were designed to catch the unwary foot.

Beyond the wood they came to a broken slope with bushes and outcrops of rock, and Daniele went down as agilely as a gazelle, leaving Feeny to slither about and curse as he tried to keep up; he had expected rough going, and he reckoned himself pretty handy, but this was too steep and rugged to be amusing – not at Daniele's pace.

Peter Pastranou would no doubt enjoy it. He still got a kick out of pitting himself against obstacles; he liked doing it the hard way. All Joe Feeny could hope was that when he came to make the return trip it would be in daylight – then perhaps he wouldn't have to progress so often on the seat of his pants. And risk breaking both legs.

After squirming their way down into a steep valley, where they had to cling to tufts of grass to avoid accelerating out of control below, they followed a winding country road that looked too narrow to take any wheeled traffic except one at a time and then only with the maximum of caution. They crossed a stone hump-backed bridge that spanned a trickle of a stream coming down from the hills. It was a relief to be moving more or less on level ground for a while.

'Isn't there a shorter route?' said Feeny. 'We've gone a hell of a long way round, it seems to me.'

'The best way I know,' said Daniele. 'Nobody seen us since we left Maddalena.'

It was true enough. Feeny adjusted his

rucksack which was beginning to cut into his shoulders mercilessly – there was damn-all in it, but its weight had increased intolerably. He refused Daniele's offer of help, mostly because the offer was made with a sly grin, as from a professional to an amateur.

When they left the road about half a mile along, then the real climbing began, up the side of a ravine with few holds and a lousy surface, no two yards being on the same level. They fought a zigzag battle with knees and elbows for the first stretch; it became a little better higher up, and Daniele allowed them a short rest, during which Feeny didn't dare unsling his rucksack because he didn't think he'd ever get it back on again.

They had no conversation; the night didn't feel chilly any longer, and Feeny was gratified to see that Daniele's pudgy face was streaming with sweat, so that he didn't have to feel all that much inferior.

When Feeny reached into his pocket and brought out his cigarettes, Daniele caught his hand and said a very emphatic no – too risky there.

'There's nobody within miles of us,' said Feeny. But he put the cigarettes away, and sucked in some more mountain air. It would

be a pity to spoil all those elaborate pre-
cautions.

In all they had been travelling a little over
two hours since they had left the van, and
now they were making faster progress, and
they could feel the mountain winds tugging
at them.

'Just up there, mister,' said Daniele. *'Casa
dei Vento* – the house of the winds ... bloody
awful winds here in the winter.'

'I can believe that,' said Joe Feeny.

5

Feeny could see nothing. He followed Daniele up. And before they had gone another
fifty yards they were challenged – a man
with a shot-gun just appeared from a clump
of bushes, and they both halted.

Softly Daniele announced, 'I bring the
Englishman ... you keep a good watch,
Angelo...'

They were instructed to advance. There
was some friendly back-slapping. Angelo
looked almost square in build; very young
and very tough, in a woollen cap and dark

trousers and windcheater. He poked Danielle in the belly with the butt of his gun, and much of the Italian was beyond Feeny, but he could guess that it was scurrilous on both sides. They were passed on.

Set among the dark trees that hid it until one stood right in front of it, on a little lip of flat terrain that might have been carved out of the dark hillside, there was a low stone-built cottage, where no lights shone; nothing very pretentious or comfortable. This was the *Casa dei Vento,* the house of the winds, formerly a hunting-lodge high in the hills, now the refuge of a hunted man.

Angelo had reported that Missounis was awake and waiting for them. Daniele tapped on the solid wooden door and pushed it open. There was a curtain covering it inside, and they had to push it aside to get into the small room and the soft light from an oil lamp. There was going to be no glimmer of light showing outside.

George Missounis sat by the dying embers of a wood fire, with one leg propped on a low stool. He was a slight man, with a tired face and untidy russet hair. He wore a plaid shirt and dark slacks. The sandy stubble on his chin made him look very much an invalid who needed hope and fresh air. When he got up he had to lean on a stick.

He smiled at Feeny and offered his hand. 'I nearly gave you up for the night...'

'It's no Sunday afternoon stroll,' said Feeny. 'How's the leg?'

'Mending, slowly,' said Missounis. 'Have a good trip?'

Feeny let his rucksack slip to the floor. 'Not very hilarious. We almost got ourselves jumped by one of the Greeks – Daniele knew him.'

'Demetriades,' said Daniele, 'at San Bartolomeo; he had a little accident later.'

Missounis nodded. 'You'll want food... Demetriades, that will have them wondering, I didn't know they were so near.'

'You know they took Piero?' said Feeny.

'Time we were moving,' said Missounis. He limped into the small kitchen next door; there was an oil stove; water came from a pump out in the back; there was no indoor sanitation – the house of the winds was for sheltering in, not living.

Missounis got the stove going and put on some coffee; he took an earthenware bowl with ten large eggs, and used them all in an omelette; there was coarse bread and strong cheese, and a bottle of *Dolceacqua*.

'I finished the last of the cognac a couple of days ago,' said Missounis. 'My apologies; we are not exactly equipped for entertaining – if you knew how sick I am of eggs and cheese. Did you find out how much Demetriades knew?'

'No chance,' said Feeny. 'He had us cold, in the pub. Maddalena says he's been there before – she clobbered him for us with her frying pan, otherwise we'd have been in a mess. There wasn't any time to put pressure on him; we had to dump him.'

'I doubt if he would have talked,' said Missounis.

'Not gonna talk any more now,' said Daniele with some satisfaction.

'You made him safe?' said Missounis.

'Safe enough,' said Daniele.

'And nobody saw you with him?' said Missounis.

'Only Maddalena,' said Feeny.

'Then that's all right,' said Missounis. 'But I'd still feel happier if we knew what brought Demetriades up there–'

'And what information he passed down the line,' said Feeny. 'They won't find him in a hurry, if we have any luck, but there'll be somebody after him soon.'

'When you've finished,' Missounis said to

92

Daniele, 'you might relieve Angelo for a while … we're a little thin on the ground since we moved up here, and now we've lost Piero.'

'Anybody been around?' said Feeny.

'Nobody,' said Missounis. 'But it could happen any day, we've been lucky.'

'And careful,' said Feeny. 'It's a good spot.'

George Missounis smiled, rubbing the stubble on his chin. 'I've been here long enough.'

Daniele finished the last of the bottle of *Dolceacqua,* belched, wiped his mouth with the back of his hand, and went out.

'A character, that one,' said Feeny. 'He doesn't look dangerous.'

'The soul of a brigand,' said Missounis, 'which is what we need here.'

Feeny undid the waistband of his trousers, and loosened the money belt. 'I gave some to Daniele for Piero's girl,' he said. 'I've brought lire, some dollars, and the rest in fivers.'

'We'll change the fivers into lire,' said Missounis. 'We can't use English notes around here without attracting attention, Pastranou should know that, and we're getting low on food. When is he coming?'

'Early next week,' said Feeny. 'There isn't

much we can do while you have a duff leg, George – they're all looking for a limping man.'

'So I wait,' said Missounis. 'If you were a betting man, what odds would you give me? There's something I didn't mention – there was a helicopter buzzing around across the valley, yesterday, morning and afternoon. That might tie in with Demetriades being at San Bartolomeo. I think we might be running out of time.'

He limped over to the fire and threw on more logs; the wooden shutters rattled in the night wind.

'How would you like to go back to England with a genuine English identity?' said Feeny. 'In a car with Ellen driving you? And a British passport? Right through the customs on this side and all the police checks, sitting nice and comfortably beside Ellen? No question of a limping George Missounis, just another English tourist on the way home?'

'Tell me,' said Missounis.

'Ellen found someone who could double for you,' said Feeny. 'A real dummy, George.'

'But does this man know what he's letting himself in for?' said Missounis. 'Changing identities with me?'

94

Feeny smiled. 'He doesn't know; he thinks Ellen has fallen for him. It was her idea.'

'So what happens to him when we've made the switch?' said Missounis.

'Are you worried?' said Feeny. 'It's you or him.'

Missounis sat in a chair, arranged his injured leg more comfortably on the stool. 'Now let me have the details,' he said. 'It sounds cheeky enough to be possible.'

'We think it's worth trying,' said Feeny. 'That's really why I came. Ellen picked up this mug, a Sam Harris, and he could well be your twin brother – same build and colouring, but he's not very bright, at least not as bright as he thinks he is–'

Missounis grinned and looked a lot younger. 'Thanks very much ... but do go on.'

Joe Feeny told him. And by the time he had finished, George Missounis was finding little to object to. The matter of the final disposal of one Sam Harris didn't figure much in the discussion. He was to be the dummy, and as such of no importance.

Sleeping accommodation at the *Casa dei Vento* was limited, two bedrooms with bunk beds and little in the way of bedding; there was an earth closet at the back. Joe Feeny was bone-weary, but slept little because of the chill in the air and the sounds of the wind moaning around.

In the morning Daniele took off alone down into the valley to locate Anna, Piero's girl, and coax her away from the Saluzzo district; he would also, he said, pick up any news about Piero – and the police, particularly the police and what they appeared to be doing.

'Don't let them grab you,' said Missounis, and Daniele made it abundantly clear that he had no opinion at all of the *Prefettura* and the Greek Secret Police. Bastards, all of them.

It was mid-morning when the helicopter arrived, and they heard its clatter even before they could see it, chopping method-ically around the sky, low enough to be a real danger if they had been outside and moving on the open slope in front of the cottage, or if there had been any smoke from the wood fire. Missounis had used the oil stove that morning, and the fire wasn't to be lit until dark. Angelo was outside with his shot-gun, but he would be invisible.

The helicopter was still in the vicinity when they saw Angelo standing up, and there was somebody with him. It was clear that Angelo was trying to stop the visitor from coming closer.

'It's a girl,' said Feeny and glanced at Missounis. 'Are you expecting anybody?'

'That's a damn silly question!' Missounis snapped. He was limping to the door. Feeny reached it first and opened it. Angelo was obviously trying to drag the girl under cover, and she was just as obviously resisting. While they watched the girl wrenched herself free and stumbled a few yards up the slope, then Angelo got her round the legs and pulled her down, and they heard the girl shouting.

She wore jeans and a dark jersey and carried a small pack on her back and her short blonde hair flipped about wildly as she fought.

'If that damned chopper sees them,' said Missounis.

Feeny ran out and down the slope. 'Okay, Angelo!' he shouted. 'Let her up...'

The girl kicked Angelo in the belly, rolled free and stood up, panting; she had a small neat face and her blue eyes were snapping with anger.

97

'Are you English? My God, I've heard about Italian men but this is the limit – that ape tried to rape me!'

The girl dusted herself off; she looked to be in the early twenties.

Acutely aware of the sound of the helicopter, Feeny said, 'I'm sorry he was rough with you, he was only trying to stop you trespassing … I'm afraid it's all private property up here.'

'I saw no signs,' said the girl bluntly. 'You're a bit feudal round here, aren't you? Armed guards and all that jazz!'

'I'm sorry,' said Feeny. 'I hope he didn't hurt you.'

He was trying to edge the girl back into the cover of the nearest bushes, but she wasn't having any, she was glaring at Angelo.

'If you lay a hand on me again I'll ruin you for life, Romeo – understand? *Capito?*'

Angelo grinned and said nothing. The sound of the helicopter had momentarily faded.

'Now perhaps you wouldn't mind going back,' said Feeny as politely as he could manage. 'I'm terribly sorry this happened–'

'You might at least invite a girl in for a coffee – is that your place up there?' She had seen Missounis in the doorway. Angelo had retired back to the cover of his bush.

'I could do with a wash,' said the girl, 'after wrestling with your bodyguard. What are you running up here anyway, a branch office of the Mafia?' She waved at Missounis in the door, and began to walk up towards him. Feeny could think of no way of heading her off without another fight.

'I say,' he called out after her, 'you can't go up there.'

She smiled back at him over her shoulder, and kept on walking so that he had to hurry to catch up with him.

'Do please listen,' he said, and when he touched her arm she shrugged him off.

'What's happened to all this celebrated European hospitality?' she said.

There was no sight or sign of the helicopter now. Perhaps they hadn't been seen after all.

'What makes you so nervous?' said the girl. 'I'm the one who ought to be scared, and I'm not, just curious … and I don't for a minute swallow that stuff about this being private property – I've been camping out around here for days now, and this is the first time I've been threatened with a gun.'

'Angelo's a bit too zealous,' said Feeny lamely.

'You can say that again and set it to music.' She gave Feeny a quick shrewd look. 'You really are bothered, aren't you?'

George Missounis came down to meet them, smiling politely, his limp barely evident. 'I must apologise for the unfortunate mishap.'

The girl stared at him, blue eyes wide. 'So that's what it was; you could have fooled me – that ape down there has a gun. Didn't you notice?'

'A dreadful way to greet such a charming visitor,' said Missounis. 'Do forgive us.'

'Another Englishman,' she said. 'I expected mountain bandits at least. What in the world are you two doing up here with an armed guard?'

'It does look pretty awful,' Missounis agreed, smiling, 'but it's not as bad as that … we just weren't expecting visitors, and Angelo interprets his instructions too literally… I hope he didn't frighten you too much?'

'An item for my memoirs,' she said.

They had reached the cottage, and she took in its surroundings with an approving eye. 'If you're looking for a tenant for this I'd like to head the list, it would suit me fine.'

'I'm afraid that wouldn't be possible,' said Missounis very pleasantly.

'Too bad,' said the girl. 'If I couldn't write here I couldn't write anywhere.'

'You are a writer?' said Missounis. 'That's very interesting–'

'Betty Drake,' she said. 'You've never heard of me, so you don't have to pretend. I'm from San Francisco, doing Europe on foot.'

'George Parker,' said Missounis, 'and this is my friend Joe Green, both from London, on holiday.'

She looked at Joe Feeny/Green. 'That chopper just now,' she said, 'why were you scared of it?'

'Was I?' said Feeny.

'He was in a bad crash some months ago,' said Missounis. 'The noise of an aircraft upsets him still, doesn't it, Joe?'

'Always,' said Joe Feeny. 'I'll get over it.'

'Just another military helicopter on a training flight,' said Missounis. 'We get a lot of them up here. Would you care for some coffee, Miss Drake?'

'I thought you'd never mention it,' she said.

They went into the cottage, and Feeny left the girl with Missounis while he made coffee in the kitchen. He kept the door open, and he heard her explaining that she had been sleeping rough for a couple of nights, as though it were the most natural thing in the world for a young girl on her own.

She had walked and hitched her way round Sicily, and up the length of Italy, mostly alone, it appeared. Switzerland might come next before the end of the summer, but she was in no hurry, and she didn't seem to be short of money. Papa Drake back home in San Francisco and the good old American Express were seeing to that whenever she ran short.

Feeny was bringing in the coffee with some fruit and whatever biscuits he could find, when Missounis asked her if she had included Greece in her wanderings.

'Next summer, maybe,' she said, 'and Turkey and Iran...'

A much-travelled young lady, and one clearly able to look after herself. Intelligent, observant, nobody's fool ... and far from welcome at the *Casa dei Vento*.

She wanted to know how they spent their time up there, and Missounis gave her the picture of a pair of English eccentrics who preferred to be off the beaten track, and so on … and perhaps she believed the fiction of Joe Feeny as a convalescent. She knew London a little, and that was a safe enough topic, and Missounis flogged it on as far as he could.

Later she wanted to use the bathroom which they didn't have. 'You're really roughing it,' she said when she saw the primitive facilities. 'When I hit a town of any size I head straight for the four-star hotel, the best I can find. You'd be surprised how many of them don't want to let me in until I wave a few dollars … I suppose I couldn't have a wash?'

Feeny drew water from the pump and put it on the oil stove in the largest pot they had. Missounis brought her a towel, the only clean one they had.

'I'll see you get a mention in the Michelin Guide,' she said. 'What's the name of this place anyway?'

'Just a cottage,' said Missounis. 'Where did you stay last night? There isn't any village within miles of us.'

'Somewhere down there in the valley,' she said. 'Under a nice dry bush…'

While the water was heating she casually slipped her jersey over her head. She wore no bra and needed none. Her breasts were

neat and high, her back was a smooth un-
broken tan, and she hadn't allowed them
time to withdraw.

'You won't mind if I rinse out a few bits
and pieces,' she said. 'They'll soon dry.'

She was standing with one hand on the
zipper of her jeans, half-turned to them, and
she smiled very fetchingly. 'I thought you
might be a pair of English queens, but I see
you're not ... so okay, fellers, no free show
this morning ... evaporate.'

They went out and Missounis very carefully closed the door, beckoned to Feeny
and they both went out to the front, in the
open.

'What the hell do we do with her now?'
said Missounis. 'She's a smart girl, too
damn smart ... we don't want her here.'

'We can't push her off a mountain,' said
Feeny. 'I wonder if they saw her from the
chopper?'

'We'll get the answer to that pretty soon,'
said Missounis. 'This couldn't have happened at a worse time, an inquisitive girl
hanging around, asking questions and
getting ideas.'

'You think she believed us?' said Feeny.

'Would you?' said Missounis. 'A pair of
eccentric English pansies, my God.'

104

Feeny grinned, watching the sky for the helicopter. Through the open doorway and across the living-room came the sound of Miss Betty Drake's voice, happy and tuneful.

'She'll talk,' said Missounis. 'She'll yap about us and Angelo with his blasted gun, and she'll probably do it to the wrong people in some country pub around here … can't you imagine it?'

'So we chat her up nicely and send her on her way,' said Feeny. 'And keep our fingers crossed. She's a dolly bird.'

'She's a bloody nuisance,' said Missounis. 'She's dangerous. Why did she have to turn up here now?'

'We've been lucky so far,' Feeny pointed out. 'There must be hundreds like her, hitching about the place. It's the season for them, George, and we just happened to have caught one.'

'She's a writer, and she's too damned observant,' said Missounis. 'She'll talk, if she gets the chance–'

Joe Feeny stared at him and shook his head. 'If I can guess what you're thinking you'd better forget it.'

George Missounis put on his obstinate look. 'So?'

'Not another little accident,' said Feeny. 'She's not from the police. I believe she just had the bad luck to run into us here.'

'I hope you have a solution,' said Missounis. 'It's my neck and my liberty we're talking about – if we had Peter Pastranou with us I don't think he'd hesitate.'

Very quietly Feeny said, 'We removed Demetriades, and I didn't like it very much, but he was a pro and he knew the risks ... also he had the drop on us. This is different, and I won't have any share in it. There's plenty of the day left and I could find my way out of it if I had to.'

Missounis smiled without enjoyment. 'You must agree she's dangerous?'

'Inconvenient,' said Feeny. 'We have aroused her interest, naturally. Invite her to stop for lunch, give her the gentlemanly treatment, George ... she's been knocking around. Hell, we can't be the only odd characters she's met in her travels. Let's play ourselves down a bit. If she'd like to stop the night, we have a spare bed–'

'Are you serious?' said Missounis. 'That would be asking for trouble.'

'Put it to her, see what she says.'

'I haven't seen a woman for I don't know how long,' said Missounis slowly.

'She might see it as a romantic situation,' said Feeny. 'She's no wandering maiden, and a little loving might allay her suspicions.'

'I begin to like it,' said Missounis.

'I thought you would,' said Feeny. 'A little old-fashioned seduction, no rape... I leave it with you.'

6

Miss Betty Drake came out to them, looking bright and perky, her blonde hair shining; she still wore the jeans, but now they were clean, and she had put on a clean jersey, pale blue although a little rumpled from her bag. She was a pretty girl and ready to be admired and entertained as a pretty girl should be.

She smiled at the two of them impartially. 'That feels a heap better; nothing like soap and water after living rough. I've cleaned up your kitchen, gentlemen. I gather you don't have any domestic help?'

'Up here?' said George Missounis. 'Not a hope. We have to pig it, but it makes a change after living in London.'

She gazed around at the magnificent view. 'I can imagine that, I must say you have chosen a lovely place, how in the world did you find it?'

'A friend of mine,' said Missounis. 'You'll stop for lunch, won't you? There really isn't an inn within walking distance, and you must be tired of eating under a hedge, we'd love to have you with us, wouldn't we, Joe?'

'Rather,' said Feeny. 'I'm getting fed up with the sight of George's face across the table, and that's a fact.'

She laughed, and looked from one to the other. 'You're being very kind, I must say–'

'Give us a chance to make up for the ghastly way you were received,' said Missounis.

'Where are you making for next?' said Feeny.

'You tell me,' she said humorously, 'I'm the stranger around here. I'm supposed to land up at Turin eventually. I promised to call on some family friends near there, but I'm not in any hurry.'

'Then that's settled,' said Missounis.

'You do improve on closer acquaintance, the two of you,' she said bluntly. 'At first I thought there must be some kind of mystery about you – I mean that great lump down there with a gun … it did rather intrigue me, a couple of Englishmen living up here in the mountains–'

'You'll find us terribly dull after the exciting life you've been leading,' said Missounis. 'Just a pair of fugitives from the stress of modern living.'

'Rather like me,' she said. 'Only I prefer to keep moving. I see you don't have any radio?'

'No radio,' said Feeny. 'We don't miss it, or the papers or the television.'

'A complete rest cure,' she said. 'I haven't heard any news myself for ages. Plenty of time for that when I'm at home. I do like listening to the talk of the country-people I meet, that's the real news for my money … they have time to talk and I have time to listen.'

'Isn't it a bit dangerous wandering about on your own?' said Feeny with much earnestness.

'You sound like my Papa,' she said cheerfully. 'I've had some fairly explicit propositions that I don't think he would care to hear about.'

'I can believe that,' said Missounis.

'Thank you,' she said sweetly, 'but nobody

gets from me what I don't choose to give, not even an overweight Hamburg merchant banker with the longest Mercedes I've ever seen.'

'Thereby hangs a tale,' said Feeny.

'The latest offer I had was from a policeman,' she said. 'Two nights ago, not far from here. He was on a motor bike. Young and quite a dishy specimen. I had some trouble brushing him off in the end, I thought he was going to run me in for not co-operating.'

'Very difficult,' said Feeny. 'Mobile police are rather scarce in these parts.'

'Not to my knowledge,' she said. 'I seem to be running into them wherever I go.'

Feeny and Missounis exchanged glances, but Betty Drake's manner didn't suggest that she had anything on her mind.

'How long have you been here?' she asked.

'A few weeks,' said Missounis. 'Time doesn't matter very much up here.'

She squinted knowingly at him and then at Feeny. 'You can't be married, either of you – am I right?'

'Free as air, both of us,' said Joe Feeny.

'You look healthy and normal,' she said. 'You like living like this? Honestly?'

'You find it strange?' said Missounis.

'It still puzzles me a bit,' she said. 'It's like going into a retreat in a monastery or some place like that. You can't have many visitors, it's so remote.'

'You're the first,' said Feeny, 'and all the more welcome. I've never thought of George as any kind of a monk, believe me!' And George Missounis grinned accordingly.

They had an early lunch, mostly tinned stuff, with some fruit brought up by Daniele the previous day, and the presence of their guest gave it an unusual festive air, and the helicopter didn't return.

George Missounis did his best, but she wouldn't stop the night, and early in the bright afternoon sun they saw her on her way down the slope. Missounis had warned Angelo off and he remained invisible.

'Now we're wide open,' said Missounis. 'She isn't stupid, she'll be wondering about us – we don't fit the landscape, and she asked too many questions for my comfort.'

He stood for a long time staring down the way she had gone, and he was still sure they had made a mistake in letting her go. They wrangled about it in the course of the afternoon; not too amicably. Some hours later Angelo appeared; he had taken it on himself to trail the lady, and he reported that she had gone on down the valley. He was confident she hadn't noticed him. George Missounis cussed him fluently for taking such a chance which did little to improve the general atmosphere.

The afternoon clouded over and towards evening the wind got up, driving them indoors. Missounis got out the radio he had hidden under his bunk, and tried to pick up a local news programme from Turin, but there was no item of any interest to them, and the reception was poor. At nightfall there was a sudden spatter of rain against the shutters, and they thought of Miss Betty Drake somewhere under a bush down in the valley, probably regretting that she hadn't accepted their invitation for the night.

'Let's hope she doesn't meet another amorous policeman,' said Missounis. 'If she does and she talks we might have somebody knocking at our front door before the night is over.'

'I don't think that's very likely,' said Feeny. He had found a deck of cards and was engaged in some involved game of his own devising.

'I'm a realist and I've been here long enough,' said Missounis. 'We should never have let her go like that. I've come too far now to let myself be tripped up by any wandering tramp of a girl.'

Feeny went on with his game.

They didn't expect Daniele until the next day. It proved to be a wild and windy night, and Joe Feeny wondered what it would be like in the middle of winter; it was no surprise that the place had been long abandoned. It was excellent for their immediate purpose … but not to live in for long.

It was midday when Daniele came up the slope and even looked a little travel worn.

'That's one bastard of a walk,' he said, 'and it don't get any shorter.'

He followed them into the cottage. He had a haversack over his shoulder. He unslung it and dumped it on the table.

'I got some ham, coffee, sugar, tinned milk,' he said. 'I fixed it okay with Anna, put her on a coach to Turin … she's gonna have a kid, she says. Piero's, she says. I didn't have no luck with Piero, couldn't get to him, they got some awkward cops down in Saluzzo, and I didn't want to hang around or I might have got tossed inside myself. I never seen so many coppers.'

'Busy?' said Missounis.

113

'All over the place,' said Daniele. He grinned. 'They haven't found Demetriades.'

'We've had the helicopter back,' said Missounis. 'And a visitor.'

'So I hear,' said Daniele. 'She was down at Giovanni's place last night, talking about a couple of English nuts she met up in the mountains... I hear she's moved on now.'

'I wonder?' said Missounis. 'What did Giovanni say about her?'

'No business of his,' said Daniele easily. 'He don't meddle outside his own business; he's one smart boy.'

'I hope you're right,' said Missounis. 'That girl was a damned nuisance, turning up here.'

'Young enough,' said Daniele with a slow grin. 'I know where she was heading. Like me to pick her up?'

'And then what?' said Feeny sharply.

Daniele put on an innocent look. 'I bring her back here and she don't talk.'

'No,' said Feeny.

'We're being chivalrous,' said Missounis.

Feeny stared hard at him for a moment, then said, 'She's gone. When you've had some food, Daniele, you can take me back.'

Daniele waited for other instructions from Missounis. There were none, so he set about

114

getting himself something to eat. He had been well paid for what he had been doing, but he was beginning to have doubts about their chances of getting George Missounis out, and he had a feeling that all was not going well at the *Casa dei Vento*.

As Daniele saw it, there were now too many coppers in the area, and that was always bad news. Daniele had little regard for most uniformed police, with their squad cars and radios, but he knew there were situations in which the coppers were almost sure to win in the end, and this might be one of them. From the look on his face, he thought Missounis felt the same as he did.

As he chewed some of the ham he had brought, Daniele was deciding that he wouldn't be making the trip again in a hurry. He would deliver Feeny back and then see how it shaped up. He would have felt better if old Pastranou had come – now there was a man who knew what he was doing, a man who didn't have to pretend to be an English gentleman ... he would have known what to do with that American girl, he would have fixed her good.

In the afternoon Feeny and Daniele started down the slope, and they made good time in the bright sun, mostly downhill. They needed no rest periods, and they met nobody, either in the valley or on the hillside. The only incident was when the helicopter came skittering round a hill a few hundred feet up, and they both dived under a bush and lay still for long minutes until the clattering had died away.

'That's not the one they were using this morning,' said Feeny.

'Lot of mountains round here,' said Daniele. 'They won't see nothing; it's those road blocks we got to watch out for ... you still got that little gun?'

Feeny undid his holster and took it off. 'I won't be needing it now,' he said, and held it out.

Daniele scraped a hole in the loose earth under the bush and hid the gun in its holster. If he wanted it later he could pick it up when it was safe, and get a price for it.

They continued their trek, fast and purposeful, and Feeny had no complaints. Daniele had brought the van nearer this time, in the over-grown entrance of what had once been a quarry of sorts at the end of a rough stony track. They racketed down to San Bartolomeo in the late afternoon.

They left the van by the inn yard as before,

and went in across the yard. Maddalena had seen them and she met them before they could open her back door, and there was no welcome in her face.

In an urgent whisper she told them that the police had already been there that morning, asking questions, many questions, about the Greek Demetriades.

'You go,' she said quickly. 'You don't come back here...'

'I'm sorry,' said Feeny lamely. 'We didn't want to get you into any trouble–'

'I tell them nothing,' she said. 'But I know they come back soon ... so you go – I do not know you. You have never been in here.' And she shut the door.

They got out of San Bartolomeo quickly and neither of them said anything for a few dusty miles.

'If and when they find Demetriades,' said Feeny, 'there'll be a stink back there. They know he was there; they'll find somebody in the village who saw him...'

'They will get nothing out of Maddalena,' said Daniele.

'They can make it awkward for her,' said Feeny.

'Bleeding awkward all round,' said Daniele without much concern. 'We dumped Demetriades fifteen miles away, Maddalena don't drive a car, so how they gonna connect her with a dead copper in a busted car all that way off? It don't link up, long as she keeps her mouth shut. That lousy Greek, I bet he been hanging out his ear in every pub in the district.'

'Maybe,' said Feeny.

'They stir up trouble everywhere,' said Daniele, 'lousy coppers. Nothing we can do now to help Maddalena. We gotta get ourselves clear. Correct?'

It was the truth. And they both knew it. So they bundled off down the mountain road at a handy speed.

It was dark before they came down to Alassio, and they ran slap into a road block before they knew it was there, so there was no time for Daniele to turn off. They were ordered out of the van and searched there on the roadside – searched and interrogated, in the light of powerful torches, and Joe Feeny was happy that he had got rid of the little gun because he knew he couldn't have talked himself out of this.

He presented himself as another hitch-hiking tourist, very ready to co-operate with the authorities, with just enough Italian to get by. A decent amenable character with a passport that was in order and sufficient money. Seeing their beautiful country on foot, he had been wandering from village to village in the mountains, and now he was on the way back home.

They bought it; they were quite polite with him. But they were rougher with Daniele and he had the wisdom not to show any resentment, even when they poked about in the back of the obviously empty van without saying what they were looking for.

He had been up in the hills delivering stuff from the family market garden near Albenga. They could ask anybody in the town – everybody knew him there, they had a good business, the best, and so on.

One of the mobile police made some sour comments on the state of Daniele's tyres, and he promised faithfully to have them changed as soon as he got home.

They were passed through, and when they were safe Daniele said, 'Fascist bastards, sonsabitches ... you don't reckon they were looking for us?'

'They couldn't be that sloppy,' said Feeny. 'They're a long way from George Missounis; they've got a hell of a lot of roads to cover.'

Daniele dropped Feeny at the bus station in Alassio, and then drove along the coast to Albenga. There was in fact a market garden, and it would have been reasonably prosperous if Daniele had ever given it regular attention. In his frequent absences it was run by his widowed sister, a sad-faced woman who never ceased to complain of her shiftless brother who never told her where he was going or what he was doing. But she was an excellent cook, and Daniele could always shut his ears to her nagging.

That evening Feeny caught a bus along to Porto Maurizio, and in the bus he overhead talk about an unusually daring jewel robbery in one of the plush hotels along the coast. Something like this happened every season when the rich visitors had arrived, so that would explain all the police business – he hoped, and he felt easier.

He spent a solitary night in the same modest place as before, and the next morning he was on the bus across to the border. The Customs check at the *Ponte san Luigi* was rather more thorough than when he had come in, but he was happy to notice that everybody seemed to be getting the same treatment, and he had no trouble.

He was in London early that afternoon, and put in a call from the airport and told Peter Pastranou to expect him. He took a taxi to the Hammersmith flat, and Pastranou was waiting for him, wearing one of his gentlemanly velvet jackets with the air of a benign connoisseur of the utmost respectability.

Feeny was still wearing his rucksack.

'You should have left that somewhere, Joe,' said Pastranou. 'People will be thinking I am dealing with street hawkers or tramps.' He was smiling as he spoke, but the rebuke was there.

Feeny unslung the rucksack and dropped it to the floor. 'Very amusing,' he said. 'I'm afraid I wasn't thinking of your professional image.' He dropped into a chair and stretched his legs. 'I've had it up to here, Peter. I don't think I want to make that trip again.'

Pastranou went over to the cabinet. 'You need a drink,' he said over his shoulder. 'Name it.'

'Brandy,' said Feeny, and Pastranou poured for both of them and brought the drinks over.

'Difficult?' said Pastranou.

'Not what I expected,' said Feeny. 'Nothing like as snug. The police are getting too close now, and he isn't reacting in the right

121

way ... he's more touchy than I thought he would be.'

'He is part-Greek,' said Pastranou. 'He is a young man who is used to action. He has the true Greek temperament, Joe, and the spirit. There is little of the Anglo-Saxon in George.'

Slowly Feeny savoured his brandy. 'I wouldn't know about that, I'm just bog-trotting Irish, but I wouldn't put my money on him.'

Pastranou thrust out his lower lip thoughtfully. 'It is not your money that is at risk, fortunately, or your neck. What did he think of the idea in general?'

'He thinks it will work, now,' said Feeny. 'I sold it to him all right—'

'Which is why I sent you,' Pastranou interrupted.

'He's walking pretty well,' said Feeny. 'I think he's ready to try anything, and from what I saw of the set-up you'll have to hurry. They've been checking the area with helicopters; it isn't safe to move around until dark. On the way up there we ran into one of the Greeks, a snooper named Demetriades, and we had to eliminate him.'

Pastranou's smile was gentleness itself. 'Few will mourn that one.'

'Daniele did it. We were in a bit of a jam,' said Feeny. 'I didn't like it much.'

'You took a gun,' Pastranou reminded him. 'You were prepared to look after yourself, Joe, so you should not distress yourself over one Greek policeman.' He smiled. 'You should consider it a bonus that you had Daniele with you.'

'I didn't like the way it was done,' said Feeny. 'It was an execution, and in cold blood.'

'Secret police expect to die violently; it is in the nature of their work,' said Pastranou. 'I knew that Demetriades; he would not weep for you or George Missounis. It was done efficiently?'

'Very,' said Feeny. 'They may not find the body for a long time.'

'Then why should we worry?' said Pastranou gently.

'They seem to know George is still in the area,' said Feeny. 'You'll have to be quick, and you'll need a hell of a lot of luck to get him out.'

'I am like Napoleon, I make my own luck,' said Pastranou.

Feeny stood up. 'I seem to remember he lost.'

'You go and take a bath while I have some

food ready for you,' said Pastranou. 'You are tired, Joe. The good news that you bring is that George is fit to move now. We will talk about it later when you are fresh.'

Feeny had drifted to the door; he knew his way round the flat. 'Everything all right at this end?' he said.

'Ellen will be glad to hear that you have returned,' said Pastranou. 'She will be with us this evening.'

'Good,' said Feeny.

'Joe,' said Pastranou, 'when you talk to her you will be careful what you say, no matter what you feel, you understand?'

'She's going, I'm not,' said Feeny. 'I wouldn't think of talking out of turn.'

'That would be sensible.' There was a chilling expression on Pastranou's face. Un-civilised.

'I think you're on a loser this time,' said Feeny. 'But if anybody can pull it off it's you–'

'I am happy to enjoy your confidence,' said Pastranou.

Feeny went across the corridor to the bathroom. Peter Pastranou could rough it when it was necessary, but not in his own flat – everything there was right, and the bathroom was in keeping with the rest; there was an electric vibro-massage gadget to cope with Pastranou's weight problem, and Feeny gave himself a work-out after a long reflective soak. He knew the time had come to be making some private plans of his own. He had done what Pastranou had engaged him to do, and he was pretty sure it was the last time.

Peter Pastranou acted the attentive host until Feeny had finished eating, then he took a long envelope out of his pocket and slid it over the table.

'Tomorrow, Joe,' he said, 'or very soon after, you should travel for a while, relax yourself...'

Feeny took the envelope. There was no need to look inside – Pastranou always paid well.

'Marching orders?'

'You expected them,' said Pastranou softly. 'We will be in touch again later.'

'Of course,' said Feeny. 'Always happy to be of service.'

'It would be unwise if you were to talk to Ellen on your own before you leave,' said Pastranou. 'I would know of it, she is a straightforward girl, Joe, she could hide nothing about her concern for George if you said anything to unsettle her.'

'You needn't spell it out,' said Feeny. 'She doesn't know what she's letting herself in for. I think she should be told before she starts.'

Pastranou smiled. 'What a pity you thought it necessary to start an *affaire* with her. I know you have slept with her, Joe, and I know George Missounis would not like to know about that … we Greeks still preserve a regard for the honour of our women.'

Feeny stared at him. 'I'm not sorry it happened. She's a nice girl when she's given the chance… I suppose Missounis will approve of what you're getting her to do with that tick Harris? Hell, you have odd ideas about honour; you're just using her, and in a pretty lousy way.'

'She knows what she is doing,' said Pastranou. 'It was her idea, she is not a child.'

'Then I hope Missounis will appreciate what it's costing her,' said Feeny. 'You don't imagine she enjoys being with Harris, do you?'

'Leave it with George Missounis,' said Pastranou.

'So you're going to liquidate the poor bastard,' said Feeny. 'I think I'll take a long fishing trip.'

'Very wise of you,' said Pastranou.

'You know what I think?' said Feeny. 'I don't think George Missounis is worth it, and that's my honest opinion.'

Pastranou's smile was bland. 'You are no judge of that, Joe.'

'Just an errand boy,' said Feeny. 'I know.'

'But a very good one,' said Pastranou. 'You have discretion, and that is most important.'

Feeny stood up. 'I won't forget.'

'So be here late this evening,' said Pastranou. 'You will tell her George is well and hopeful; you will convince her that much of our success will depend on her. It is very good for a woman to feel she is needed.'

Feeny nodded. 'Somebody is being conned, and it isn't only that poor mug Harris. See you tonight.' He went out quietly.

Peter Pastranou sat for a while; he was not worried. He thought he was a sound judge of character. There was a flaw in Feeny's make-up – he might imagine he had some kind of a tenderness for Ellen, but he wouldn't do anything about it. He had taken the money and he had said his piece, and that would be enough to satisfy his conscience. The world was full of Joe Feeny's. Small men with a price.

PART TWO

7

Betty Drake didn't have to sleep rough that night, for which she was later very thankful when the rain came on. On a twisty lane in a deep valley she had the good luck to be overtaken by an elderly vehicle. She thumbed it down and the driver obligingly stopped and invited her up.

He wore washed-out blue velvet trousers, and a frilly shirt that once was white, one gold earring, lots of curly black hair, gorgeous teeth, and the kind of smile that would warn any prudent maiden to keep her legs crossed and her elbows at the ready. He was sixty if he was a day, Betty decided. One of nature's triers. Full of git-up-and-go.

The vehicle was a museum piece, a van of sorts, with bottles in the back. He was, he announced, Professor Antonio Buffo, the celebrated herbal healer, the one and only originator of Buffo's Elixir, Buffo's Balsam, and so forth … perhaps the Signorina had heard of him?

'God's gift to suffering humanity,' said

Betty. 'Sure, everybody's heard of you, Professor. How's trade?'

'Not what it was,' said the Professor, shrugging sadly. 'Country people have little faith any more, they spend their money in the shops – I spit on all chemicals and all their families!'

'Rugged,' agreed Betty. 'Too much education, that's the bane of our civilisation.'

Twice in the next mile or so she had to remove his hand from her thigh. No offence on either side. The Professor was a philosopher – some did and some didn't, and a man didn't know which was which until he tried. The Signorina understood, and was not offended? She was a woman of the world and a very pretty one.

In explicit terms, in a serious tone and without touching her or looking at her, the Professor told her precisely what he would like to do with her, but he kept on driving.

'If you sold those bottles as eloquently as you sell your potency, Professor, you'd make a quick fortune,' she told him. 'Sorry, I'm not in the market.'

He accepted it like a gentleman. He was no menace. Where was he heading? San Bartolomeo by nightfall. Was there an inn? There was, and it was run by a very good friend of his, Signorina Maddalena Mostacini.

'You go on being a nice old grandad and I'll buy you a drink when we get there,' said Betty cheerfully. 'Several drinks, okay? Maybe supper.'

It was dark when they reached the village, and beginning to rain, but Betty thought the inn looked just what she needed: food and a bedroom, even a bath?

Maddalena Mostacini gave the Professor a fairly frigid reception, which suggested no tender memories on her side. She was remembering the bar bill he had left without paying five months ago, and she would make sure he didn't try it on again.

The Professor ordered a bottle of *Dolceacqua*. Betty paid and asked about accommodation for the night, for herself. Maddalena liked the look of her. An American. Not many girls found their way up to San Bartolomeo on their own. It would be somebody to talk to.

Before she took Betty up to show her the room, she fixed the Professor with a sharp eye and told him she wished to have a word with him later, and the Professor knew what she meant. He would wait, of course.

Maddalena took Betty upstairs and showed her the room. There was a large double bed, carpets, a dressing-table with a mirror – an actual mirror! Betty grimaced at her reflection and ran her hand through her tousled hair.

'Did you ever see such a fright?' She dumped her pack on a chair. 'I'm almost too ashamed to be here.'

Maddalena smiled. 'You are having a walking vacation?'

'You could call it that,' said Betty, grinning.

'You have come far?' said Maddalena politely.

'Originally San Francisco,' said Betty.

'I have heard of it,' said Maddalena, and they both laughed.

'Sorry,' said Betty. 'I mean I've been over here most of the summer, walking.'

'Very health-making,' said Maddalena. 'That one downstairs is no friend of yours, I think?'

'Gave me a lift on the road,' said Betty. 'A pick-up. I was glad to get it, to tell you the truth … if he wants anything to eat will you put it on my account?'

Maddalena said she surely would. She showed Betty the bathroom with the hot water heated by the new electric heater, of which she was so proud. She gave her a rough towel, told her that there would be food when she was ready, and went down to the bar.

Professor Antonio Buffo had gone, of course. He had a very bad memory for small accounts, here and there. She would nail him the next time. In the meantime she was going over in her mind the visit from the police that morning. Important policemen in dark suits, not pleasant or friendly. Asking, asking … and perhaps not believing what she had told them, that she did not recall a visitor – Demetriades.

They had also questioned the few men in the bar – the same questions, and she did not think they had been happy with the answers they had received, the men of San Bartolomeo being very stupid and slow in front of officials.

The evening trade began, mostly men she knew from the village, including Dino, their own policeman; he was young and he was ambitious, wishing for a chance to bring himself to the notice of those others in the dark suits who drove large cars. It was not his habit to hang about the inn in the evening, except when he was after some information.

He drank little, he was playing the detective, watching and listening. They laughed at him behind his back, the others who had things to hide from the law.

Maddalena wasn't laughing, she was waiting for him to go. He made her uneasy. The police in a bar was never a good thing. She served an excellent supper to her American guest who had made herself quite at home with the men in the bar, talking to them and laughing with them, telling them amusing stories about walking through Italy, buying them drinks. She had plenty of money, she was of a rich family in America, Maddalena could tell that.

There were these two crazy Englishmen she had met squatting on a mountain in a little shack, and guarded by a guy with a gun! Imagine – a gun! As phoney as hell, the pair of them … now why in the name of sanity would they want to hide all the way up there? Sure they were hiding, they couldn't fool Betty Drake…

Dino had moved in and Maddalena tried in vain to catch Betty's eye and warn her.

'Signorina,' said Dino formally, 'these men, did they give you their names perhaps?'

Betty looked at him. She had gathered that he must be the local law man. He looked young and a bit stupid.

'They called themselves Joe Green and George Parker,' she said. 'From London, they said.'

Dino nodded profoundly. 'Was one of them limping a little?'

'That's right,' said Betty. 'He tried to hide it, but I saw all right – he did have a slight limp ... listen, I was only making a joke of it, they were just a pair of oddballs ... you don't mean they were criminals? Why, they invited me to stop the night with them–'

Most of the male audience grinned appreciatively. The invitation made good sense to them.

Betty laughed. 'I talk too much ... I was just building the thing up–'

'Signorina,' said Dino with much gravity, 'you must come with me; it is police business.'

'Lordy, lordy,' said Betty, 'you really shouldn't take me seriously, officer ... those weren't desperate criminals, even if one of them did have a limp – or have I run into something?'

'You will come with me,' said Dino. 'It will be unpleasant for you if you do not.'

'Now wait a minute,' said Betty Drake. 'I am an American citizen with an American passport. Are you putting me under arrest? That sounded very much like a threat to me.'

She gazed at the men and got nods all round. 'Well now, officer,' she said placidly, 'if you're going to haul me off to the caboose you'll have to charge me with some offence and I will of course demand to be put in touch with the American Consul, wherever he may be in this neck of the woods. I haven't broken any laws that I know of. Correct?'

Dino frowned. He had never taken an American woman into custody before. Americans had money and some of them were influential enough to make serious trouble, which would do a country police-man no good. This one was no vagrant, in spite of her clothes; she had been spending good money on drinks for the sniggering peasants all the evening; he had noted her wallet, as a good detective should, and it was far from empty.

Clearly she was an educated girl, and she was not showing him much respect.

'I do not threaten you, Signorina,' he said stiffly.

'Good for you,' said Betty. 'I am a peaceful visitor in your beautiful country.'

She was making fun of him again, and the others around her also knew it.

'You will remain here,' said Dino severely. 'You will not leave until I return.'

'Sheriff,' she said, 'or whatever you call yourself, I have a nice room reserved upstairs and I intend to occupy it. I am very tired, so don't hurry back. Tomorrow will do...'

Dino wagged a finger at her. 'I will report to my superiors, Signorina.'

'You do that,' said Betty, quite unabashed.

Dino stamped out, a little red around the neck, and the derisive laughter that followed his exit would have justified him in putting the lot of them under arrest. But the village jail had only two cells, and they would only make him look foolish. More discreet to pretend he hadn't heard.

It was pouring with rain now, and he was soaked before he reached his police house on the edge of the village. He would telephone Saluzzo and let them see what an alert policeman there was in San Bartolomeo. They would send a car with officers who would know how to deal with this insolent American, and in the meantime Dino would post himself on duty outside the inn so that the American girl did not escape.

Dino had been recently married, and his Julia was waiting and ready for bed, ready in every way in a nightdress that hid nothing of her. There were some sharp words before Dino got into his small office where the telephone was.

Julia came after him and stood there, and that didn't help his concentration, because she knew well what the sight of those large and beautiful breasts did to him.

The line was bad, the operator was asleep, Saluzzo was engaged, everything was conspiring against Dino. Julia perched her ample haunches on the edge of his desk and encouragingly put his free hand where only a loving husband's hand should go.

Dino groaned with frustration. Julia nibbled his ear, ending with a sharp bite just to remind him. When he finally made contact with the Saluzzo station it was Benedetti he talked to, and he knew he was going to get little satisfaction: Benedetti had been the police heavyweight boxing champion, and he had been hit around the head so often that nothing made too much sense to him any more. He had won medals and cups, he was a Sergeant, and he should have been pensioned years ago.

He thought little of Dino's report; it made

no sense to him mostly because he didn't listen properly, and also because his scrambled intelligence was occupied with the recent news that the Volkswagen driven by the Greek agent Demetriades had been found in a ravine with the body of the Greek.

All the ranking officials had left Saluzzo to investigate, with cars and a breakdown truck, and Benedetti was still feeling aggrieved that he had not been included.

When Dino heard where the wreckage of the Volkswagen had been found, he said with exasperation, 'They must have passed through here, they should have stopped and taken me with them ... it is almost in my district–'

'Mebbe they thought they could just manage without you,' said Benedetti.

'It is highly irregular,' said Dino.

'So you go and complain to them,' said Benedetti. 'See what good it does you, son.'

'But what am I to do about this American girl?' said Dino in some desperation. 'She has important information–'

'Bet she got something else as well,' said Benedetti. 'Bounce her in a cell and see what you find.'

'That also would be irregular,' said Dino virtuously. His Julia was as good as in his lap

141

now, her arms about his neck and her mouth still nibbling all over his face.

'All American girls take it,' said Benedetti. 'Give yourself a treat, boy–'

Julia grabbed the telephone. 'I heard that!' she shouted. 'You are a great pig, Sergeant Benedetti!'

Benedetti was laughing as he broke the connection. Dino tried to soothe Julia.

'You come to bed,' she insisted. 'Now … you are my husband.'

He assured her she was his one and only love, but he had to go out again on duty.

'Duty!' she spat at him, those eloquent breasts jumping around under her night-dress. 'You talk to me of duty? Your duty is in bed with me! What is this I hear about this American woman? You go to her, is that what you do? She is better for you, perhaps? American slut!'

In full cry she followed him out, beautiful and full of noise. He went out to the shed where his oilskins hung, and where he kept his sole means of transport, the Lambretta. He put the oilskins on over his already soaked clothes, because he knew that if she got him up to the bedroom to change his clothes he would never get out again that night.

The rain was lessening, but the Lambretta refused to start, as usual. Over and over he had asked for something more reliable. Once the winter had come it was suicide to ride a Lambretta on some of those mountain roads. They even quibbled each month about his mileage claim.

Julia shouted at him from the door that he needn't bother to come back, and the light from the kitchen behind her made those curves and valleys he knew so well doubly inviting. He was still tinkering with the Lambretta when she slammed the door. A girl with spirit who needed much loving.

In due course Dino stamped some life into the Lambretta and wobbled out and into the village. They should have stopped for him when they came through. It showed how little they thought of him.

It would open their eyes when they heard what he had to tell them. Maybe they would change their minds about him and give him the promotion he deserved. That fool Benedetti had been vague about where they had found the Volkswagen, but Dino was sure he would find it eventually – they would have to admit that he was an example to his colleagues.

They were always preaching about showing initiative and taking responsibility.

The rain came down again, sheets of it; he had forgotten his goggles, and the Lambretta's headlamp was as unreliable as its engine; the cumbersome oilskin flapped and crackled in the wind, and didn't help Dino's balance.

He made slow progress, and after a little more than a mile he quite lost the road on a bad bend and finished up in the ditch with the Lambretta on top of him. No matter what he did to it, the engine refused to respond any more. So he began to push it back the way he had come.

He was a very weary young man when he reached the village. The inn was all in darkness. He selected a place where he could watch back and front of the inn. He had all the village to himself now. Dino, the Sleepless All-Seeing Eye.

After a while he became aware of his saturated trousers and soaked shoes. At two o'clock in the morning, in the rain, San Bartolomeo had little to attract, and Dino's zeal began to evaporate. But what he was really waiting for was the chance to step out into their headlights, hold the police convoy up, and make them listen to him.

He had rubber boots in the shed, and his

gardening trousers would at least be dry. He trundled the Lambretta back. He'd be quick and quiet and Julia wouldn't know he had returned.

He was standing in the kitchen minus his wet trousers when he heard the cars coming through, and when he got out to the edge of the square he was just in time to see the tail lights of the breakdown truck bumping down the hill out of San Bartolomeo.

So it had to be the telephone once more. Benedetti was in the canteen, naturally, but Dino did at last manage to find somebody who would listen to him. He went upstairs and found Julia had locked him out, but she had left a blanket on the floor.

It was early in the morning and Betty Drake was still sleeping, in the raw as was her habit whenever possible. A very agitated Maddalena roused her and told her there were the police downstairs wanting her. Not Dino. An inspector, and others as important. She was to dress and come down quickly.

Betty made them wait a full twenty minutes, since she thought it unlikely that she would have the use of a bathroom with hot water in the immediate future. Maddalena brought her up some coffee and begged her to hurry or they would come up for her.

Betty glanced at her inquisitively. 'You look worried ... you know something about these two Englishmen I met?'

'I know of them,' said Maddalena carefully. 'One of them is a Greek...'

'A friend of yours?'

'I have never met him,' said Maddalena. 'There are friends of mine who have been helping him to avoid the police ... police from Greece as well.'

'So I spoke out of turn,' said Betty. 'I'm sorry. I seem to have fouled it up.'

Maddalena shrugged despondently. 'How could you know? You are a stranger, you are not from these parts.'

'I'm an old blabber-mouth,' said Betty. 'Perhaps I'll forget where the place is – I have a lousy sense of direction.'

'You will make trouble for yourself,' said Maddalena. 'You should not concern yourself with this, it is a bad affair. Very dangerous now.'

Maddalena knew that they had found the body of the Greek, Demetriades, and his wrecked car, so there would be little hope that Daniele would risk coming up to San Bartolomeo ... Daniele had a way of hearing about these things, and he was her only way of getting a warning through. He would not come, so there was nothing she could do.

'In these hills we are seldom friends with the police,' she said to Betty. 'It is political … it has always been our habit…'

'I'm not too fond of some of the fuzz myself,' said Betty, 'and that goes for the good old United States as well. I suppose this isn't a Mafia thing?'

'If it were,' said Maddalena, 'it would have a better hope of success. The *Cosa Nostra* has no need of an amateur like me; they would have got him out of here—'

'I saw two of them,' said Betty. 'They both said they were English and they sounded like it—'

'There was a visitor from England,' said Maddalena. 'He was here, he left yesterday … the other is the one they look for, he is Greek, and I think now they will capture him—'

The bedroom door was flung open. The Italian Inspector was young and tough, and not inclined to wait any longer. The Signorina had her clothes on. Good. She would come with him.

When Betty began her patter about being a lawful American citizen and was she being arrested the Inspector cut her short. She could argue that with his superiors at Saluzzo. He escorted her down.

With her in the back of the police car was a man in civilian clothes to whom she was not introduced and who said nothing at all to her. A silent ghoul with flinty eyes and a rat-trap of a mouth. He smelt of toilet water and needed a shave. A Greek, she surmised. Thumbscrews. Chinese water-torture. Those dirty things they did with electrodes… Betty Drake began to feel far from optimistic about her ability to fool them for long.

Her sense of direction was more than okay – you didn't choose to wander about Europe on foot if you couldn't tell north from a hole in the road, and the police would know that.

Greek policemen swanning around in the mountains with the Italian police, that surely suggested this 'George' who limped and tried to hide it was one hell of an important criminal. She thought of asking the Inspector what he had done, but decided it might be safer not to know too much.

'Political,' Maddalena had said, and that might cover a lot of highly unpleasant ground. Betty was remembering the helicopter the day before and how nervous they had acted, and that ape with the gun.

If she had accepted their invitation for the night, 'George' would have been the one – all the signs had been there … the old animal heat ready to generate. On both sides.

A man on the run, that would have been a new experience, and not one to retail to the old folks at home. She was hoping he would get away with it, whatever it was.

At Saluzzo they whipped her straight inside an office, where she was grilled politely but quite exhaustively, and some at least of her charming interrogators were police officers of importance, not locals. They knew how to handle a girl like Betty Drake, and she soon decided there was no sense in trying to fool with them.

Why should she? This 'George' who figured so largely in the conversation appeared to be a desperate character. She was assured he was no ordinary crook.

What else could she do but co-operate? There was a large map of the district which she was invited to examine, with profes-sional assistance.

'I think I'd recognise the place if I got near it again,' she said. 'There weren't any roads…'

There was another conference among the boss interrogators. The names they had quoted meant nothing to Betty. All hills and valleys. It all looked the same on a map.

Perhaps the Signorina would be willing to try to lead them near the area? Retrace the route she had taken?

She was amenable. Directing a police search for a badly wanted criminal in rough country – now that would be something to talk about back home.

They gave her some excellent coffee, and within half an hour the convoy was winding out of Saluzzo, four car loads, and quite an amount of artillery, she noted. She had a camera, but they told her to leave it behind. Too bad.

Angelo saw the party down below late in the afternoon. Some in uniform with the sun glinting on their weapons, and he recognised the girl with the fair hair – the girl George should have let him deal with … now here she was, leading the police. The bitch.

Angelo bolted up the slope, bending double. The scheming bitch. George always kept a haversack ready with rations against an emergency – an emergency like this.

'Police down in the valley! About a dozen

150

– that girl is down there with them showing them the way!' said Angelo.

George grabbed the haversack. 'Any dogs?'

'No,' said Angelo. 'I saw none...'

They left by the back door and ran into the edge of the wood. Angelo was leading and he was quick and decisive. There were no paths, but he had rehearsed this route, and in daylight they could make good time.

They had left no fire going, so the police couldn't tell just how long they had been gone. Dogs would have made all the difference.

'You should have left that girl to me,' said Angelo.

'I expected something like this,' said Missounis.

Angelo declared vehemently what he would like to do to that girl, and it was not gentlemanly.

'Will we make it to the cave before dark?' said Missounis.

'We have to,' said Angelo. 'We got six or seven miles of bad country to do ... we might not find it in the dark.'

'You find it and you can buy that farm you want,' said Missounis. 'That's a promise.'

'I find it,' said Angelo. 'You okay?'

'I'm with you,' said George Missounis. His leg was aching and he had trouble keeping pace with Angelo's steady lope over the broken ground.

They had followed the wood round the side of the hill, now they were working their way across and down into a steep valley that was closed at each end. There was plenty of good cover, but they had to pull themselves out of the valley, and Angelo spent some time surveying the best route. He had a natural eye for terrain, and whatever he did Missounis copied.

They allowed themselves a few short rests without any fear now of being overtaken or seen – there were no roads here or houses, only a succession of tricky escarpments, acres of thick scrub, sometimes a tiny mountain stream tumbling from rock to rock. They wrestled themselves out of one steep valley into another; nowhere could they keep to any line. A helicopter could have got there in a few minutes, but the journey took them just over four hours.

Angelo's navigation was excellent, and the sun was dropping below the distant mountains when they came to what they were seeking, a natural fissure in the rocks hidden behind some scrub. It was dry and deep enough to let them risk a fire clear of the entrance, and with careful rationing they had enough food for about two days.

'Tomorrow,' said Angelo confidently, 'I look around, I get us food okay...'

Daniele was the real problem. They had to find some way of restoring contact with him. The situation was difficult, but not desperate. As George Missounis saw it, it was a temporary recession, no more than that. And for Angelo, spending a few nights sleeping on the ground in a dry cave with a nice wood fire was no kind of hardship.

8

'You didn't think I was going to allow myself to be hauled around America behind both my aged parents, did you? Be your age, Ellen,' said Kitty Dobell. 'This is my scene, here, duckie, and I'm doing very nicely, thank you. So who needs America?'

'I bet they made a fuss,' said Ellen. 'They took it for granted that you'd be going with them.'

Kitty smiled sweetly. 'I'm educating them not to take me for granted, and I don't think I'm doing too badly.'

They were in the 'study', and Ellen was tidying some papers after a long day's typing. 'I thought the house was being closed,' she said.

'It is,' said Kitty. 'I am being permitted to share a flat in London, and if you don't think that's a resounding victory you don't know my stuffy parents.'

'I work here,' said Ellen. 'Remember? I can't imagine how you talked your father round.'

'He was easy,' said Kitty. 'I told him I didn't want to miss any classes at the art school – I gave a beautiful performance. It was a bit tougher with the old lady; she has a nasty suspicious mind when you get down to it.'

'She's female and she knows you,' said Ellen, 'or she's beginning to.'

'The girl I'm going to bunk with is Antonia Piggott. She's definitely square, Oxford and so on, works in the Treasury. A professional virgin, and her father is on some city boards with mine, so that makes her okay.'

'Hardly your type,' said Ellen. 'I didn't know you were all that keen on your art classes.'

'Who knows?' said Kitty vaguely. 'I may even find I have talent. I must try it sometime. Are you all set for your trip?'

Ellen nodded and slipped the folders into the filing cabinet. 'Pretty well,' she said.

'You're still seeing that funny little man,' said Kitty. 'What was his name? Sam Harris?'

Ellen stood up and straightened her skirt; she had been typing most of the afternoon, and now it was after six. She was meeting Sam at eight; she had to bathe and change, and she wanted to phone Peter Pastranou before she saw Sam.

'Honestly, I don't understand what you can possibly see in a man like that,' said Kitty. 'You can't like him, Ellen–'

'No accounting for tastes,' said Ellen lightly. 'He amuses me; in any case, it's strictly business.'

Kitty grinned, came over and ruffled Ellen's hair. 'You'll have to do better than that to snub me. Is he going with you? To the villa, I mean?'

'What an idea,' said Ellen, smiling. 'That wouldn't be at all proper, would it?'

'Be more fun,' said Kitty, 'and don't give me that lady-like stuff.'

'I wouldn't dream of it,' said Ellen. 'You're

much too sharp.'

Kitty followed her out into the corridor. Mr and Mrs Dobell were dining in London. In two days they would be taking off for New York, and at the prospect of what lay ahead of her Ellen had been sleeping badly. She had a sudden impulse to round on Kitty and tell her for God's sake to mind her own business. But she knew that would be unwise. The only safe way was to treat it all as a bit of a joke.

'That's a long way to go just to be on your own,' said Kitty.

'I hear there are some luscious hunks of manhood on the Italian Riviera,' said Ellen.

Kitty glanced at her wonderingly. 'You've been reading the wrong Sunday papers. They're all wolves, they'll take little you for all you've got, see if they don't.'

'Well that'll give us something to chat about when I get back. Now I really must rush, Kitty–'

Kitty shook her head. 'He must have something, your little Sam, but I can't put a name to it. Is he one of those sex athletes?'

'Dirty talk will get you nowhere,' said Ellen, smiling as pleasantly as she could manage.

'Gets me plenty of interesting places,' said

Kitty. 'You'd be surprised.'

'I doubt it,' said Ellen and went down the stairs. She was relieved to see that Kitty wasn't following. She bathed and dressed in record time, and she was wishing it was Joe Feeny she was going to be with, because Joe hadn't been exactly communicative about George since he had come back, and there were still plenty of things she wanted to ask him about George, and she had the uneasy feeling that Joe was keeping something back. Also Peter Pastranou always seemed to be there when she wanted to talk to Joe, and she had begun to think it was deliberate, which didn't make her feel too happy.

Maybe she was getting fanciful, but if Joe was avoiding her she wanted to know why. It wasn't much good trying to talk to Pastranou because he seldom gave out with any details, except that George's leg was better and that he was not fit to travel, and all the rest of it was under control, Peter Pastranou's control.

It would be mad to quarrel with Pastranou now. She couldn't afford it if they wanted George to get out. Pastranou said he could do it, and she had her part.

And Sam Harris? What was going to happen to him over there? Pastranou wouldn't discuss that bit of it, except to say that

Harris would be all right, once he had served their purpose ... she had to choose between George and Sam Harris? Suppose it came to that? Sam was harmless. He had such a notion of himself that it was really pitiful when she thought of how they were going to use him.

So far he was being terribly proper and respectful towards her. He was a simple soul, for all his brashness, and if she let herself think about him too often – and what they were going to do to him – she ended by disliking herself with unusual intensity.

But being sorry in advance for Sam Harris wasn't going to help now. Pastranou had made it clear that if they didn't move George within a week the police would probably get him, and that must never happen.

She had the use of the black Mercedes 220 for the evening, and as she backed it out of the garage she was relieved to note that the Porsche was out as well. The less she saw of Kitty in the next two days the better she would like it. In the village she rang Joe's number and got no reply. It was disappointing because she did want to talk to him, and she thought he would have been expecting her to call.

She rang Pastranou. Routine, as he had instructed her. She said everything was all right with her, she was on her way to meet Sam.

'Keep him interested,' said Pastranou. It was odd how dirty he could make that sound.

'Is Joe with you?' she asked abruptly.

'No,' he said. 'You have something on your mind, little Ellen? Let me deal with it.'

'I wanted Joe,' she said. 'I want to talk to him.'

'Talk to me,' said Pastranou. 'I have given Joe a holiday; he has been working too hard and he needed a rest.'

'I see,' she said. 'When is he coming back?'

'I wish I could tell you that,' said Pastranou. 'I believe he is in Dublin but I have no address ... we will not be needing him again.'

So Joe had been paid off. That much was clear.

'Amuse your Sam this evening,' said Pastranou.

'I wish we hadn't started it this way,' she said.

'Now you are being female,' said Pastranou, 'and it is much too late to be changing your mind, everything is in hand–'

'I'm not changing my mind,' she said with

159

emphasis. 'But I'm still bothered about Sam Harris afterwards–'

'Weigh him against George,' said Pastranou. 'You know what happens to political prisoners in Greece – we have talked of this, Ellen, and George Missounis is no ordinary man.'

'You don't have to tell me that,' she said.

'This Harris is nothing but a convenience,' said Pastranou. 'You found him. Now we are going to use him, so you will forget what you feel.'

'I wish I could,' she said.

'You will, when you see George.'

When she met Sam he noticed that she was edgy, and he thought maybe she was getting nervous about having him along on the trip. Because the way Sam saw it, this was an open invitation to help himself, asking him to go with her. She would know what to expect.

Hell, it was only common sense; no bird in her right mind could expect a bloke to go all that way just to sit in the sunshine.

She said she was all right, just a bit tired – Mrs Dobell had been keeping her extra busy, she explained.

Sam also had a problem, but he kept it to himself because of its delicate nature. The ageing daughter of joy from whom he'd taken the basement flat and to whom he now owed a fair slice of back rent, had inconsiderately returned for a brief visit from Majorca, and was demanding the arrears.

Sam could have handled that with his usual finesse and it wouldn't have cost him more than a load of sweet talking, but the awkward bitch had brought her 'protector' with her to see justice done, and although this old lecher was fifteen years older than Sam, he was also some four stone heavier with one of those faces you could strike a match on, and when he tapped Sam on the chest his finger damn near went through to Sam's backbone.

To part with actual cash just at this point offended all Sam's theories of living. He was about to leave the country, so he drew a cheque on one of several accounts that had run dry long ago, and while they were out taking it to the bank, Sam had packed his gear and removed himself before they had time to discover how high that cheque would bounce.

He needed a cheap quiet place just for a few nights. He had a number of addresses, but he decided to move out into unworked territory where he wouldn't run into anybody he knew. He found what he wanted in Chertsey, which was far enough out for his purpose, a guest-house that had seen better days with a deaf landlady and one fattish maid who didn't wash too often. He posed as a travelling 'rep'. The food was lousy and all he ever saw of the other inmates were two elderly female teachers who talked in whispers and largely ignored his existence, which suited Sam fine.

Ellen had never shown any real curiosity about where he lived, and he had never told her – if she had seen the dump in Notting Hill it would have scared her off for good. Now he was handy to her, and that was okay.

Apart from a little necking he hadn't tried anything on her. There was no hurry, and that good old Mediterranean sunshine would do the trick.

Now and then, but not too often, he did wonder just why she had picked on him. In that job of hers she must come up against plenty of likely characters who wouldn't exactly throw up at the prospect of spending a holiday abroad with her.

He had tried to prod her into talking

about her men friends, but either he had been too clumsy or she was too shy. So maybe she was actually getting fond of him. It did Sam good to think that. And why not? He was no cripple, and he knew how to handle most women. This was going to be a bonus.

The night before they were due to leave, Ellen let him come up to the cottage with her. Mr and Mrs Dobell were already in New York, and the house was to be closed up the next day.

It was Sam's idea to talk Ellen into showing him around the place. It was still quite early, and according to Sam's philosophy it was never a waste of time to know for sure where items of value might be, and how conveniently they might be reached, if the occasion arose, as it so seldom did – unless you kept both eyes open.

Langley House, the Dobell place, must be loaded with gear that a sharp character might just happen to slip into his pocket in passing; gear that wouldn't be missed for a long time, so nobody could tell when it had been knocked off. It was asking for it.

They'd had a couple of small drinks, and Sam was about to break into his patter when there was a tap on the door, and Kitty Dobell entered, the original swinging chick in black stretch pants as sexy as a thin coat of shiny paint and one of those crochet see-through jerseys that did exactly what it was intended to do; her blonde hair was tied back in a large baby-blue ribbon.

She went through the pretty business of being just a mite confused to see Sam there.

'Do forgive me, Ellen … I saw your light and thought you might be feeling lonely – so sorry.'

She made no move to shunt herself out; the white door behind her made an interesting contrast to those clinging pants. She smiled brightly. 'Do say if I'm interrupting.'

She came into the room, doing her Eartha Kitt panther stuff, just for practice and Sam wasn't missing any of it.

So Ellen had to introduce him and invite Kitty to join them and have a drink, and Kitty forthwith took the party over, nor did Sam act as though he resented the intrusion, not a bit of it.

Kitty draped herself into one corner of the chesterfield, her focus on Sam so that he knew the see-through jersey was no dud, and when the chat shifted to Ellen's trip she tried in vain to give Sam warning hints to watch his lip.

'Have you ever been to the Italian Riviera, Mr Harris?' said Kitty.

'Not yet,' said Sam, as though it just happened to be the one part of the Continent he had overlooked.

'You'll love it,' said Kitty. 'Won't he, Ellen?'

Ellen smiled thinly and made no comment.

Kitty gave her gurgling laugh and tucked her legs under as neatly as a cat. 'Oh dear,' she said, 'have I made another boobie? I mean I know you're both going, and I'm perfectly certain my aged parents wouldn't in the least mind, if they knew.'

Sam cleared his throat, and glanced at Ellen. Her face was stony.

'I won't be telling anybody,' said Kitty.

'You're a good sport,' said Sam.

Kitty was suddenly convulsed with merriment. 'I've never been called one of those before, but rest assured – your romantic secret is safe with me, and Ellen deserves a bit of fun in the sun, so who am I to spoil it?'

'You're getting the wrong idea, Kitty,' said Ellen as pleasantly as possible.

'Come off it, duckie,' said Kitty just as pleasantly. 'I think your Sam's a lucky man, and he knows it.'

'That's right,' said Sam, grinning.

'Never pass up a good thing, right?' said Kitty, glancing brightly from one to the other, but mostly at Sam. 'Nobody gets hurt, am I right? So what's the odds? It's all in the game.'

'You got something there,' said Sam who felt he had to say something because Ellen was looking down her nose.

'Pre-cisely,' said Kitty and emptied her glass for the second time. 'Are you running short of whisky, Ellen? There's plenty up at the house. Listen, why don't we all just move up there? Have ourselves a party? Music and stuff? Come on you two, let's break out–'

She got up and padded joyfully to the door, and Sam thought he'd never seen a nicer retreating view – no doubt about it, black did something extra to those slim legs.

Ellen gave him a shrug of resignation. A squabble with Kitty in this mood would get them nowhere.

'All right,' she said, 'we might as well–'

'Such wild enthusiasm,' said Kitty. 'Don't strain yourself. Sam looks like an eager boy – am I right, Sam?'

'We're right behind you,' said Sam, and they followed her out, across the dark garden and into the house, and Ellen had hold of Sam's arm just to remind him. It would have been much more sensible if she had sent him home and gone to bed herself.

'You go on up,' said Kitty, switching on the lights in the hall. 'I'll collect the booze.'

Ellen took Sam up to Kitty's sitting-room where she had her hi-fi, colour television, tape recorders, discs, and kindred gear.

'Watch your step, Sam,' said Ellen warningly. 'She's putting on an act, that's all it is, don't let it fool you...'

Sam slid an arm around her waist. 'She doesn't fool me, besides, she's only a kid.'

'Some kid,' said Ellen. 'Don't forget we have a long drive in front of us tomorrow.'

'I'm not thinking of anything else,' said Sam, which was nearly the truth. He had already noted some items that would relieve his financial embarrassment for some time to come.

Kitty arrived with an armful of bottles. Vodka, whisky, gin.

'If we had another chap we could have an orgy,' she said. 'Sam, you'll just have to share yourself out–'

'A fate worse than death,' said Sam cheerfully, which Kitty appeared to find very hilarious indeed.

The music came on; the din was deafening at first until Ellen toned it down. Kitty poured the drinks, and the party was on.

Some two exhausting hours later, when Sam got into his car for the trek back to Chertsey he was in no real condition to drive. Of the three of them, Ellen was the only sober one, and Sam had been hoping she would invite him to spend the night at her cottage. No dice. She steered him down the stairs and into his car, kissed him nicely on the cheek and told him to drive carefully.

'I'll need you all in one piece tomorrow,' she reminded him.

'I could bunk down on your couch,' said Sam. 'No trouble, baby, honest – I'm stoned ... how about it? I don't fancy that lousy drive.'

Ellen smiled and moved back from the car. 'You be a good boy and go on home, Sam, just this time–'

'Doesn't make any sense to me,' said Sam. 'Nobody would have to know–'

'Kitty would know,' said Ellen, 'and I don't want that – I still work here, Sam.'

'Okay,' he said wearily, 'have it your own

way – see you in the morning.'

As he drove carefully out into the road he was thinking that Kitty would have taken him on without a second thought; she acted stewed to the eyeballs, but she knew what it was all about. He was remembering how she had whipped off the see-through jersey to do her crazy version of the dancers in 'Top Of The Pops', bouncing those nice little Bristols practically in his mouth so that he was almost scared to look in case she knocked his eyes out. Dynamite. Her old lady would have had kittens.

Along the road he found a lay-by and got his head down for a bit. It didn't help much, and if a patrol car came along they'd book him for sure. So he drove on, and reached Chertsey without mishap.

He climbed into his solitary bed with the comforting thought that it would be different tomorrow night – in some French hotel. Cripes, it had to be, or Sam Harris wasn't the man he knew he was.

9

Ellen did the driving, down to the coast, in a Ford Escort Utility, provided by a friend of hers, she said. Sam's car had been left at the cottage, and when they left at mid-morning there had been no sign of Kitty; her Porsche was in the garage, so Kitty was still in bed.

Peter Pastranou crossed on the same car-ferry, driving a dusty Fiat; he wore shabby English tweeds, he had an untidy grey moustache, and his passport said he was a Cypriot restaurateur, domiciled in London, Peter Pyannotis by name; visiting his widowed sister in Genoa.

When he came face to face with Ellen on the ferry each looked straight through the other, and Sam hadn't a clue. There was a small swell running, and Sam was in no condition to notice anything outside himself.

Ellen had planned their route: it would be over seven hundred miles down to the border, and they would spend two nights on the way. She had done the drive before, she said, and Sam was happy to leave the first stretch to her. She was the best woman driver he had ever ridden with, and the crazy French traffic didn't seem to bother her one little bit. She knew the lingo and didn't have to search about for directions.

They spent the first night near Reims, at a hotel she knew. So they had two single rooms – she was tired and Sam was amenable because his stomach was still heaving about. He knew he wouldn't be able to do himself justice. So he agreed to act the gent.

They made an early start the next morning, and since Sam was feeling more like his confident self he took over some of the driving. He had no reason to note the Fiat that kept close to them all the morning, and Ellen did some very efficient map-reading.

When he cussed the traffic she told him that the route by way of Lyons was even worse in the summer months. She fed him cigarettes at intervals, so that he began to feel in charge of the situation. She was a good girl to have around on a trip like this. No fussing, no beefing. And when they stopped to fill up she knew the right words and got them quick attention, French garage hands being as susceptible as any other male citizens to a pretty girl, and that morning Ellen was looking really pretty.

She had sandwiches and cartons of milk made up for them at their hotel, so they didn't have to waste any time looking for a wayside place to eat. They had a picnic of sorts on a little piece of grass clear of the road, while the Fiat waited for them a few hundred yards down – missing a meal meant nothing to Peter Pastranou. He smoked and waited and eventually tagged on behind.

In the afternoon Ellen drove, and Sam had to admit that she was better than he was on those roads, and like most men Sam considered his own driving was superlatively good. Another pleasant feature was that Ellen had taken care of their travelling expenses, and so far Sam had been riding free – half way across France without having to put his hand in his pocket, and with a lovely dolly like Ellen to do the hard work.

Not many blokes could have latched on to a bonus as fabulous as this. It took the authentic Sam Harris touch. Like winning the treble chance.

When they stopped for the second night at Chambéry, Sam made no demur when he heard that Ellen had already engaged two single rooms, and that there was nothing else available. She had been driving fast and she did look weary. He could afford to wait.

They had a good meal, and to his own surprise Sam heard himself insisting on paying for it, although Ellen told him it wasn't necessary.

'We'll have to come to some arrangement,' he said. 'I can't have you paying for everything.'

She smiled. 'Mrs Dobell gave me an extra cheque before she left, and the villa won't cost us anything, except what we choose to spend outside.'

'Fifty-fifty,' said Sam.

'We'll see,' she said. 'You won't mind if I have an early night, will you? I'm rather tired.'

'You look fine,' said Sam gallantly.

'You're rather sweet,' she said, and her face was suddenly thoughtfully fixed on his. A lamb to the slaughter. And he was trying so hard. She wouldn't want to remember any of this later.

'I'll look round the town,' he said.

'Some interesting buildings,' she said.

'You have to be kidding,' said Sam, grinning at her. 'A pub with some beer will do me for an hour or so ... or maybe one of those French night clubs.'

'In Chambéry?' She laughed, a genuine laugh. 'You can try, Sam, but I don't think you'll have much luck.'

'If there's any drinkable beer in the place I'll nose it out,' said Sam. 'They got night clubs in San Remo, I hope?'

'San Remo has everything,' she said, 'if you believe the guide books. We'll be there by tomorrow afternoon.'

'You hop up and get yourself a good sleep,' said Sam, with a wealth of meaning. 'We'll have ourselves a rave-up, right? Starting tomorrow.'

Later, after seeing him leave, she went along to the telephone. Peter Pastranou was waiting at his hotel.

'You drove well,' he said. 'Getting anxious?'

'A little.'

'Not long now,' he said. 'You can stand it.'

'Peter,' she said, 'he's being really rather pleasant, not what I was expecting–'

'Good,' interrupted Pastranou. 'That should make it simpler. See you tomorrow night.'

He rang off. She went into the hotel bar and got herself a vodka. She had promised herself that she would watch her drinking until this was done with. The vodka did

174

nothing for her. She went up to bed and lay awake for a long time.

She would almost have welcomed a visit from Sam. If he had forced himself on her then she could persuade herself to dislike him enough to go on with what she was doing ... and not feel so guilty.

And she had been the one who started it, after meeting him in that tea-shop. She felt shabby and ashamed, and helpless.

Early the next afternoon they were at the *Villa Rivarola* in San Remo. It was a pleasant property, set in a walled garden, very private and cosy. It had been built just after the first World War by a manufacturer from Genoa who had made his pile out of Army contracts, and who needed the right kind of setting to accommodate a succession of mistresses – each one younger and more expensive than her predecessor, until in the expected course of events the manufacturer over-reached himself with a statuesque blonde and embarrassingly expired in her arms.

Since then the villa had passed through a number of hands, until Mark Dobell, who had the rich man's nose for a bargain, bought it cheaply, and spent money on it to make it into a family summer residence.

There were four bedrooms, each with its own balcony and bathroom, a sun lounge, and a modern kitchen. The erotic murals that had formerly decorated the master bedroom, along with some statuettes, had long since been removed. Now the *Villa Rivarola* was highly respectable, and worth at least twice what Mr Dobell had given for it.

With the permanent fixtures there was Anna, a middle-aged local woman, who lived out but came in daily to see the place was ready for immediate habitation in case the Dobells decided to arrive without warning, as they sometimes did.

There was also a visiting gardener who kept the lawns and flowers in shape.

Anna showed no surprise when Ellen arrived in company with a man; she found it quite natural – everybody knew what English girls were like when they got away from their own sunless country, and furthermore, she liked Ellen, so she gave them both a flattering welcome, although she didn't think Ellen's Englishman would be good for much of a tip. Anna had a practised eye for the quality, and Sam Harris didn't make it.

During most of the afternoon they lounged in the garden in the shade of the lemon trees, recuperating from the drive, with iced drinks brought out to them by Anna. Sam wore his holiday gear – light blue slacks and a dark blue jersey, and Ellen wore rust-coloured shorts and a red and white striped blouse, and Sam told her she looked terrific. Which she did.

'You're nice and restful,' she said lazily. 'Did you ever see such gorgeous flowers? They grow more here than anywhere on the Riviera...'

Carnations, hyacinths, tulips – they were all one to Sam, but he had to admit that they made an impressive show.

'This is the right spot for a girl like you,' he said. 'I'd make you a present of it if it was mine.'

She smiled. 'I believe you would.'

Sam grinned. 'Always ready with the big talk, that's me...'

Later in the afternoon they drove down and looked at one of the beaches. Nice clean shining sand, yachts, some energetic water-skiers out in the bay, bright beach huts for the sun-bathers and the few swimmers; not too many kids about.

'We'll have to try it in the morning,' said Ellen. 'You swim, don't you, Sam?'

'Well, sort of,' said Sam cautiously, remembering how skinny he looked when stripped. 'I'll be quite happy under one of those jazzy beach umbrellas watching you do your stuff – that won't be any hardship, believe me.'

They strolled along one of the pleasant promenades, lined with lemon trees and eucalyptus and acacias. This wasn't Brighton or Blackpool. Even the air smelt better. Must be all those flowers.

Sam's roving eye spotted plenty of birds, and some of them were real smashers, but he was more than happy with what he had. Ellen had taken his arm, all nice and friendly. She wasn't saying much, but that was okay. Sam had plenty of words for both of them.

There was no getting away from it, the right atmosphere made a difference. This was going to be good. Maybe he was really falling for her in a big way. Now there was a thought. Why not? He could do a lot worse. She'd never want to push him around, he was sure of that … and when it came to the good old loving in the bedroom Ellen would be more than okay – Sam was sure of that as well.

They explored some of the town on foot.

A bloke and his girl, like any other couple on holiday without a care in the lovely sunshine. She showed him the Casino, and he promised her they'd give it a modest whirl one evening. He didn't care much for the massive *Forte San Tecla* by the mole, not when Ellen explained that it was used as a prison. It reminded Sam of some episodes in his past that he hoped to forget for good.

They watched a flying boat make a spectacular landing after a trip along the coast to Menton, Monaco, Nice.

'We'll have a bang at that before we go home,' said Sam. 'Looks good.'

He didn't notice her lack of enthusiasm. He was full of plans. He felt he was fit for anything. Sam Harris, on top at last. Everything bright and under control. Sam's exclusive control.

Anna took it as no insult to her cooking when she heard they would be eating out that first evening. She had made up two of the bedrooms, and confidently expected only one would be needed. She would not be arriving too early in the morning, she said as she wished them a *buona notte*.

They were dawdling along the fashionable *Via Matteotti*, and Ellen was window-

179

shopping, when Peter Pastranou appeared out of the crowd.

'Ellen,' he said, 'is it really you? What a very pleasant surprise!'

'Peter! How nice to see you!' She introduced Sam, and he gathered that this old geezer was an friend of the Dobells. He looked like a boring old bastard, name of Peter something-or-other.

He was making a big fuss over Ellen, calling her 'my dear Ellen' and patting her all the time, like some kind of an uncle with his favourite niece. He had latched on to them all right, and Ellen didn't seem to mind.

'You must both be my guests for dinner,' said Peter Pastranou. 'I insist, then you can give me all the news about the family ... will they be coming over?'

'Not yet,' said Ellen. 'They're in America.'

'Ah yes,' said Pastranou, 'now I remember, so you are taking a little holiday, just you two ... very nice, we must celebrate your arrival, and I know just the place.'

He beamed at Sam, and Sam could do nothing but fall in. They could put up with the old clot for a couple of hours. If he was a friend of the Dobell family he had to be rich, although he didn't look it. Sam never quarrelled with free food.

He took them to a restaurant where the lights were dim and the carpets thick and the table linen stiff enough to shave with. There was a menu as long as your arm. Italian chow.

'May I be permitted to choose for you?' said Pastranou. 'I frequently dine here…'

Ellen just smiled like a little girl being taken out for an evening treat, and Sam said it was okay with him – he couldn't identify steak and chips anywhere in all that fancy stuff.

The Chianti was all right, and he got on with the soup – *Minestrone alla Toscana*, because it was only vegetable soup after all. Pastranou assured them that they would enjoy the *Frutti di mare* – the fruits of the sea, assorted fish and shellfish, the speciality of the coast, but Sam had his doubts because shellfish always gave him hell and he didn't go much on the sauce.

Before the meal was over Sam was feeling distinctly uneasy, and very much regretted that he had shovelled away at the main course, *Filetti di tachine al burro,* which Pastranou had said were fillets of turkey fried in butter and in much demand. There was a *Macedonia di Frutta,* a fruit salad flavoured with liqueur, and cognac, and a cigar.

Sam didn't skip anything, he took the lot, and he knew he was making a mistake. His insides were beginning to churn over and his head was muzzy. He'd have to make a bolt for the gents soon. He was taking no part in the social chat – he might well have been sitting all by himself in that bloody room with all those food smells. Yuk. He closed his eyes and felt quite unhappy.

'Your friend does not look well,' said Pastranou to Ellen.

'Sam,' said Ellen, 'are you all right, Sam?'

He tried to focus on her but she kept drifting around.

'Sam,' she said anxiously, 'are you ill?'

He gave her a Death's Head grin, and got to his feet unsteadily.

'Feel lousy,' he mumbled. 'Must be something I ate ... excuse me...'

He lurched drunkenly across the restaurant. A waiter appeared at the opportune moment, took his arm and steered him out of sight, along a corridor and into the toilets, where Sam was noisily sick right there in the middle of the nice tiled floor before he could reach the pedestal and the basin. The waiter ran him a basin of water. Sam shoved his face in but it didn't help much.

Peter Pastranou came in and made sympathetic sounds, while Sam propped himself against the tiled wall and groaned ... all he wanted was just to be left to expire alone.

'You must have a stomach disorder,' said Pastranou.

Too bloody true. Sam wiped his face on his sleeve; there were clean towels but he couldn't be bothered.

'Gotta get inna bed,' he said.

Pastranou took him outside. Ellen had got the car waiting. The dinner party was over, evidently. Like a tormented ghost, Sam was helped into the car; he sat with both hands clutching his belly and prayed they would soon be near a toilet. Ellen drove and Pastranou insisted on coming.

Sam groaned and said he was sorry.

'You poor fellow,' said Pastranou and sounded as though he really meant it.

Ellen drove fast through the town, while Sam had a desperate feeling that it wasn't going to be fast enough because he had little control at either end ... some bloody romantic evening – it was plain murder. It made him sweat.

When they got to the villa Pastranou helped him out, and Sam was doubled over himself like a paralytic. Somebody was ramming red hot pokers through his guts.

In the hall he shook off their offers of assistance and groaned his way up the stairs. He had to scuttle the last few yards. He made it to the bathroom, but only just. His belly was on fire and he couldn't even be sick any more.

He heard Ellen tap on the bathroom door, but he wouldn't open up. She was the last person he wanted to see him in that deplorable state, so he told her to go away and leave him ... he'd be all right.

When the internal eruptions seemed to have done their worst, he found some aspirin tablets in the cabinet. He took four; they didn't want to go down.

He crawled into his bedroom, and he could have wept in sheer misery as he fumbled out of his clothes and fell on the bed in his vest. The pyjamas that were to dazzle Ellen lay under his pillow and he didn't give a damn.

Maybe he should have locked his door, but he was too weary to get up ... she would have enough sense to understand. He couldn't even reach up and put the bedside light off. He had a fit of the shivers and passed right out.

'Well that solves your problem for tonight,' said Peter Pastranou pleasantly. 'You can sleep alone.'

An expression of sudden distaste flitted over Ellen's face. 'I wasn't thinking of that,' she said.

'You feel sorry for him,' said Pastranou. 'Don't you?'

They were in the sun lounge; the sliding windows were open to the fragrant night.

'It is very beautiful here,' said Pastranou. 'I would not grudge you a romantic encounter in these surroundings, my dear Ellen, if the man happened to be worthy of you, but the one upstairs is not … and I must remind you again that you chose him.'

She drew a deep shaky breath. 'Suppose he's still ill in the morning?'

'He has had a belly ache from the food,' said Pastranou patiently. 'Nothing more than that. He has the eating habits of a pig. Would you expect anything different? You would not willingly sleep with that, would you?'

She said nothing, just stared at his smiling face.

'Now you will listen very carefully,' said Pastranou, 'because this is important. I will call tomorrow morning to ask how the

185

invalid is. You will see that he is up, and when I suggest that the three of us might take a drive in the country to admire the beautiful scenery you will find it an excellent idea; you will persuade him that it will be just what he needs; if he is reluctant you will coax him – and if you cannot do that much you should not be here. You understand?'

'All right,' she said. 'But why?'

He put an arm around her shoulders, but she wasn't responsive, so he shook her gently.

'Before I came to you this evening,' he said, 'I was with Daniele; he is now on the way to warn George that we will be on the road tomorrow. Daniele will arrange when and where we will pick George up … now are you listening to me? It is tomorrow, it must be.'

'It's too soon,' she said rapidly.

'From what Daniele tells me we have little time,' said Pastranou. 'Why do you hesitate?'

'You've never told me what is going to happen to Sam Harris afterwards,' she said. 'I want to know that, Peter. I must…'

He touched her cheek. 'He has had a pleasant free ride, so far. He cannot count with you against George, surely? You are being sentimental and that is silly in our situation, we cannot afford it – you must agree?'

'You're not going to kill him, are you?'

Smiling, Peter Pastranou lifted both hands. 'That would only complicate things.'

'I don't believe you,' she said.

'Killing is the last resort, in an emergency,' he said, like an academic lecturer to a dullish pupil. 'If you cannot accept that, you should have stayed back in England. Sometime between now and when we leave here tomorrow you will have to get his passport – that is more important to us than whether he lives or dies. Get it and have it with you.'

He squeezed her shoulder hard. 'The passport,' he repeated. 'We are all in your hands now, especially myself. You could ring the *Commissariato di Publico Sicurezza* and tell them that Peter Pastranou the Greek they are looking for is in San Remo, and they would probably pick me up before the night is out … you could do that, dear Ellen – but I think you will not.'

'No,' she said in a stony voice.

'They have some idea where the other Greek is, George Missounis. They are still searching, Ellen, never forget that … and by now they have come too close, so we hurry,

187

tomorrow, understood?'

She watched him walk over to the door. He paused. He made a nondescript figure in the doorway, in that tasteless tweed suit too heavy for the climate, the straggle of grey moustache. Nobody would notice him.

'It will all depend on you,' he said very quietly. 'It began with you, only you can now make sure of the right ending. Keep that in your mind. Forget everything else.'

'There is nothing else,' she said and her voice sounded strange because her mouth had dried.

'I sent Joe Feeny away because we had no further need of him.' The words were thrown at her across the room. 'You had a silly fondness for him, Ellen – you will not make the same mistake with that one upstairs.'

She let him see himself out. She waited a long time before she went upstairs, to stand outside Sam's room, very still and listening. She tapped on the door and there was no answer, while she argued with herself that it would be better to wait until the morning, and hope she would get a chance to take the passport. She had seen him unpack and she knew he kept it in the pocket of his jacket.

She sat on the bed in her own room and

smoked a cigarette and wished it was all over and done with. Supposing she couldn't get the passport in the morning?

She took off her shoes and tiptoed across and went into his room without any more hesitation; if she didn't do it now she never would. Her heart jumped when she saw the bedside light still on – he would think she had come for him, that she couldn't wait to be invited in. Oh God.

He didn't stir. Only his lips sloppily puffed in and out with his breathing. Saliva had dribbled on to the pillow from the corner of his mouth, his face was grey and sweaty, and she could smell the sick in the room.

Not an appetising sight, sprawled there in a vest. A sad little man. A loser. His bad luck was that he had met her in a tea shop in peaceful England, and that he happened to look just a little like George. So she had elected him, and tomorrow night he might just know why … and he wouldn't be thanking her.

His clothes were spread about the floor, his jacket on the bed. Holding her breath she knelt and felt for the passport.

If he missed it in the morning they could pretend he must have dropped it when he was being sick; they could pretend to make enquiries at the restaurant, perhaps even report it to the police.

Sam grunted as she made for the door with the passport clenched tightly to her breast. He made wet papping noises, like an infant feeding. He didn't wake. She closed the door gently and went across to her own room. She was safe. She had done it. Like a thief. She couldn't stop herself trembling.

She put the passport in her bag and hid it at the back of the fitted wardrobe. He might make a fuss in the morning, if he missed his passport, and she could only hope that Peter would be there if it happened. He was a good liar.

She took a long slow bath, but it did nothing to soothe her. When she closed her eyes in the scented water, she couldn't believe she had engineered all this. But nobody else had ... it had all begun with her.

Tomorrow she would watch Peter Pastranou very carefully all day. And she was thinking of Sam Harris as she fell asleep.

At first Daniele had not been anxious to take the trip, but Peter Pastranou had his own private brand of persuasion, and there was money to back it up.

'There will be no more after this one,' he

said. 'If you are thinking of a work permit in England, I have friends there who will be glad to arrange it for you – there is still money to be made in London by a smart man, like yourself.'

Daniele shrugged. 'I have a good business here.'

Pastranou smiled. He knew better. 'You could be running your own café in Soho, Daniele. I would back you. You will always be having trouble with the police while you are here, unless you turn respectable and spend the rest of your life selling vegetables.'

Daniele was weakening, as Pastranou knew he would.

'I ask it as a favour,' said Pastranou, and pressed a folded wedge of notes into Daniele's hand, more than Daniele could hope to earn legitimately in six months.

Before the evening had turned into night, Daniele was driving his van out to the hills. His widowed sister had given him the rough side of her tongue again: he was off gallivanting, she had all the work to do, he was a lazy good-for-nothing, and so forth.

This time in the back of the van he had some stuff – mushrooms, tomatoes, spinach, all useful camouflage if he got stopped on the road. He was just another working man making late deliveries.

He made the fastest run so far. He was stopped and checked once, and it wasn't by the same lot of police as before and they were evidently not interested in him. He was alone, and he was driving the wrong way, up into the hills, not away from them.

There was no Angelo to challenge him as he came up the slope to the *Casa dei Vento*, but that didn't bother him. It was not until he saw the open door of the cottage that he began to suspect that there had been an incident – the door was wide open and there was no light inside.

He entered very carefully. He had a small torch. They had left in a hurry. There were dirty dishes in the kitchen. He was looking for signs of a fight, bullet marks on the walls or broken glass. George and Angelo wouldn't have been taken without a battle. He saw that the emergency bag had gone, and that wasn't to be touched unless they had to run for it. There was dust everywhere, from that open door and the wind blowing in. Nobody had been here for a couple of days, he thought.

Peter Pastranou wasn't going to like this

news. It ruined everything, unless Daniele could pass on the instructions for the next day … and if he could do that he'd make sure of Pastranou's help for good, his own place in London. Money.

He knew that Angelo had fixed a bolt-hole somewhere, but he had never been there, and he only knew vaguely where it might be. So that was going to be no help in the dark. He'd never find it. He was good, but not that good.

Maddalena was the only one left. She might knew something. George and Angelo wouldn't hide themselves in a hole in the hills and do nothing.

It was just before midnight when he reached San Bartolomeo. The inn was in darkness. He tapped on the back door, tried it and heard soft steps inside, and Maddalena's voice. She opened when she heard who it was. There was a shaded lamp on the kitchen table, and Angelo was finishing a meal.

He showed no surprise at Daniele's arrival – it was what George said would happen; he had been sure Daniele would turn up soon, at the inn.

'It's tomorrow afternoon,' said Daniele. 'How is it with George?'

'Dirty and hungry.' Angelo grinned. 'I am now just dirty. We had to vanish a little quickly. I have been asking Maddalena to marry me, she is such a good cook, and I am the one to teach her about loving.'

Maddalena smiled at him. 'Finish your food, little man, and you go about your business.'

She was looking better than before, because now she was not being pestered by the police, and the American girl was no longer in the inn. They had not found the man they wanted, they had missed him by a few minutes, and now they had no idea where he was. To Maddalena all this was good.

'Old Pastranou has come,' said Daniele. 'We are to get George tomorrow afternoon.'

Angelo eyed Maddalena impudently. 'So I must leave, what a pity – I had planned a much sweeter way of passing the night.'

'Out,' said Maddalena, not offended. 'Both of you.'

They left by the back door, quietly.

10

When Sam Harris opened his eyes the morning sun was streaming in through the slatted blinds, and the bedside light was still on. He sat up very gingerly and found he had the strength to turn the light off. Gawd, what a night.

His mouth was sour, his stomach rumbled, and he was as hungry as hell. A nice strong cuppa would do as a start. Plain grub from now onwards, old cock, he promised himself. They can stuff their fancy chow.

He rolled out of bed and he wasn't paralysed. He picked up his scattered clothes, and grinned as he recollected how he had just made it to the bathroom. Talk about a panic. They'd have a good giggle about it, him and Ellen.

Anybody could have a stomach upset, especially a highly-strung bloke, like Sam.

He opened the venetian blinds and took a sniff at the morning. The sun was shining, the birds were singing, the flowers were blooming. And there she was in a tiny blue skirt and a white blouse picking the flowers and stuffing them into a large basket. Pretty as a picture on a calendar.

She saw him, waved and came over the tidy grass, smiling. 'Feeling better, Sam?'

'You look smashing,' he said. 'I'm okay.' A little too late he remembered his vest and lowered himself.

'Breakfast when you're ready,' she said. 'What do you fancy?'

'Scrambled eggs, toast, coffee,' he said.

She laughed. 'You've recovered then?'

He slapped his chest. 'Me Tarzan, you Jane.'

He withdrew into the bathroom, full of energy. It would take more than a little bilious attack to spoil this holiday. He shaved and bathed and put on some of his brightest gear. The sky would be the limit today, and then there would be tonight. And Ellen.

He fancied Ellen was acting a bit nervous as she sat and watched him deal with a fairly substantial breakfast, and put it down to her concern about his digestion.

'I'm okay now,' he assured her in the best of good spirits. 'I mucked things up a bit last night ... I never could stomach that spicy grub, know what I mean?'

196

She said she did. He was still eating when their visitor arrived. Peter Pastranou declared that he was delighted to see that the patient had made such an excellent recovery.

'I really had to call and see how you were, my dear chap. That was most unfortunate last night.' Pastranou smiled. 'I blame myself.'

'Don't give it another thought,' said Sam. This wasn't such a bad old geezer after all.

'I have an idea,' said Pastranou, turning to Ellen. 'I think a little drive up into the hills might be just the tonic our friend needs. It is a beautiful day … we might even take a little picnic … does that appeal to you both?'

Ellen nodded.

'Okay with me,' said Sam. 'I'm game for anything, it's a nice day.'

'Good,' said Pastranou. 'We will choose our food with care this time.'

'You bet we will,' said Sam with a grin.

'Plain food to keep us all happy,' said Pastranou genially. 'Rolls, mild cheese, fruit, and plenty of your excellent coffee, Ellen.'

'I'll get it ready,' she said, rising, and Sam didn't notice the odd look she gave Pastranou or the even odder expression on her face.

Pastranou excused himself and followed her out. They could hear Anna banging about upstairs with the vacuum cleaner.

'I have it,' said Ellen. 'He hasn't missed it yet.'

They went into the kitchen, and Ellen began to get the picnic stuff ready.

'We will be using the Ford,' said Pastranou. 'I will drive – you are in such a nervous state that I would not trust you to keep us on the road.'

'I'll be all right,' she said briefly.

'I will see that you are,' said Peter Pastranou, and there was no cordiality in his voice, and nothing but a chilling menace in his eyes. He needed to say no more as she went on with her preparations.

It was a beautiful morning as they drove out of the town. Ellen was on the back seat and Sam sat beside Pastranou. Past the golf course and out on to the road of Monte Bignone, along the hillsides with the glimpses of large villas set in fine gardens, Pastranou pointing out the items of interest, and being in no hurry, stopping wherever there was a view of note … a bumbling old coot, Sam decided, but harmless. They'd have to bounce him when they got back from this mystery tour. He could see Ellen wasn't enjoying it much, she wasn't saying a word.

After an hour or so on a fair sort of road, Pastranou turned off and they began to get some rough riding, and even Pastranou had to abandon his travelogue because the driving took all of his attention. They were climbing and twisting, and now and then Sam saw some nasty drops. And there wasn't much clearance on the side, just one hell of a lot a damn-all if your brakes failed.

When Pastranou pulled up and said, 'We can eat here, I think,' Sam wasn't all that sorry. He needed a bush or a large rock to attend to his bladder.

So he hopped nimbly out of the car and sauntered across to take a look, and it didn't look too promising – there was a steep slope and not much in the way of cover for a couple of hundred feet or so. He was lighting a cigarette to give it some thought, when he heard a shout behind him – Ellen shouting: 'Sam!'

He turned and he saw Peter Pastranou coming towards him and he wasn't looking a bit friendly – he had a gun and he was lifting his hand, and Sam suddenly knew he was the target, and he also knew this was no joke from the look on Pastranou's face. The old bloke must have gone off his nut, and he wasn't more than fifteen feet away.

Ellen was running, waving her arms. 'Run Sam! Run!' she was shouting. She got to Pastranou as he got Sam in his sights. She tried to grab at the gun, and Pastranou shoved her off so that she fell on her hands and knees.

And that settled Sam. He was turning to bolt down the slope and he heard the gun and something whipped past his head. He had been in plenty of trouble before this, but he'd never had anybody shooting at him so close. He lost his footing and started to tumble down the slope, and there was another shot, at least one more.

He rolled and bumped and wasn't trying to stop himself. There was coarse grass and scree that shifted under him, but there weren't any boulders to knock him silly. Where the slope lessened he had to do something, so he scrambled to his feet and didn't wait to see how near that murdering old bastard might be – he just went on leaping down, and he had enough sense left to zig-zag, and to begin picking his way because if he busted an ankle that would be the end, and Sam Harris didn't intend to finish his career on any bloody mountainside while some crazy old tick took pot shots at him.

He had got so far down now that he couldn't see the top, and he couldn't hear anything – maybe that was good ... and maybe it wasn't – there might be another way down, and a bullet could travel faster than Sam ever expected to travel, so he didn't squat to catch his breath or argue the toss with himself – keep on travelling fast, boy.

There was some handy cover down below, bushes and rocks and stuff, pretty broken up and dodgy ... Apache territory, Gawd help us. Keep on moving down. There might even be some kind of a track or a road down at the bottom.

If there was that bastard would know about it; he could drive round and cut him off. Much better to keep to the goddam jungle for a bit. Sam was no athlete, but he was sure he could lose Pastranou in the open if he had to.

He wondered how Ellen was making out. She had given him the chance to get away. If she hadn't shouted Pastranou would have put a bullet in the back of his head.

Sam shuddered at the thought. Some bleeding picnic. He squinted up at the sun, but it didn't tell him much except that it was right overhead, and he was dripping with sweat. He had some small bruises, and he had torn the legs of his trousers and the sleeves of his jacket. But he wasn't a stiff. Not bloody likely. Shaking a bit maybe, but still around.

It didn't make any sense. As friendly as you please one minute, then the moment Sam turned his back the crazy old goat came after him with a gun. Having partly recovered from his initial panic, Sam was beginning to feel the anger boil inside him, and he wasn't all that surprised to find he was grasping a solid piece of rock, just in case.

He didn't know which direction he ought to be heading in, but he knew he ought to keep clear of any roads, so he went on dodging around. His wind had come back, and he reckoned he was doing pretty good.

Now why would anybody want to shoot him? It was crazy. He was a stranger, he'd only met the bloke for the first time last night. Sam's stomach gave a sudden lurch as he realised that the whole idea of this trip had come from the man who had just now done his best to kill him, so that meant it had been planned, obviously … Sam Harris taken for the old-fashioned one-way ride!

Sam took temporary refuge under a bush because his legs all of a sudden didn't want to work any more. Paralysed by panic and why not? What the hell had Sam ever done to make himself a fair target like that? The bloke must have blown his top. All that smooth talk and then he whips a gun out behind Sam's back. Sam had another fit of the shudders at the thought.

'You are a fool!' Peter Pastranou looked down at Ellen on the road. 'You realise what you have done? I had him. He would have known nothing. Now I must find him.'

He lifted his foot as though to kick her, but changed his mind and began to trot briskly up the track.

'I hope to God you don't find him,' she shouted.

He took no notice. As he ran he was examining the slope down which Sam had tumbled, he was estimating Sam's probable line of escape, angling across the slope to the right where the cover began. Sam had gone that way.

Ellen got to her feet; she shouted something, perhaps a warning to Sam. It was instinctive. She stood on the edge of the slope, she could see nothing but the broken hillside, but she went on calling.

Pastranou had found what he wanted, an easier way down, and she watched him disappear among the rocks and bushes. He was far more agile than he looked, this was the kind of thing he had done before ... hunting people down. She didn't think Sam had a chance, unless he was very lucky and better at this than she thought, and he'd only had a few seconds start.

She was seeing the startled look on his face as he turned and saw Pastranou – it would have been cold-blooded murder, and now she knew he had intended to do this right from the beginning, and she couldn't absolve herself because she had just shut her mind to it.

She looked anxiously down into that sunlit valley, praying that Sam Harris would have all the luck he needed. She was listening for more shooting. There was none. Peter Pastranou said he killed only in an emergency. This would be one, surely. She couldn't detect any movement below. And there wasn't any way now that she could warn Sam. It was like waiting for him to be executed.

She felt sick. And guilty. As long as she lived she thought she would be seeing Sam's frightened face.

She went back to the car, but the keys had gone, Pastranou wouldn't make such a silly mistake.

Sam was about to leave the shelter of his bush, when he heard her faint shouts and he knew it had to be Ellen, and she didn't sound like a girl in distress – or maybe he wanted to hear it like that so he wouldn't have to do anything. He crept back under cover and listened some more, and she had stopped shouting.

Then he began to hear other sounds, sounds of stones shifting, up behind him. Cautious sounds that made him frightened to swallow because of the noise his dry throat made.

There was open ground down there in front of him, fifty yards or so, then what looked like more bushes, nice thick ones. That was where he ought to be, on his belly among that lot, like a rabbit. Too late now, he'd never make it.

He squirmed further into the bush and let it close down around him. He wanted to cough and sneeze, and something was tickling the back of his neck as he lay face-down, and pretty soon there were gangs of insects crawling all over him and giving him hell. He didn't think he could stand it much longer, and he could feel the sweat dribbling down behind his ears.

Sam Harris had never been so unhappy. He had been on the run before, many times, but in civilised situations, where there would be streets and buildings a smart bloke could use, and he had always known what the opposition wanted him for – something he had done they didn't care about. That was fair enough, it made a difference.

But this was clean crazy, being chased around the country by a madman with a gun … and then what had Ellen got to do with all this? A nice girl like her – he thought he'd picked himself a winner, a holiday in the sun with a doll, and now look what happened. Enough to make a bloke swear off women for good.

Pastranou had surveyed the terrain, and he felt fairly sure he knew where Harris was. That thick clump of bushes below the open ground was the likely spot, and Harris had had time to get that far, he thought. He would try to break out at the lower end of the bushes, where there was a little fissure and some more rocks. There was no movement among the bushes.

Pastranou went down across the open ground and placed himself on the flank where he could see all of it. There was a faint breeze at his back, and the bushes and the grass would be dry.

He set fire to some of the bushes on the edge and stood back to watch, then moved a little lower down to keep it all in view. Harris would have to come out; he would bolt out of the lower end, in front of the flames.

The smoke coiled and spread, shifting with the breeze very satisfactorily; the flames were jumping from bush to bush and in the right direction. All beautifully dry. Birds rose and squawked and rabbits darted out into the open. Smiling, Pastranou waited. This time there would be nobody to spoil his shot.

A clumsy way to do it, and not what Peter Pastranou had planned, but it would serve.

From the shelter of his bush, saved by that open space below, Sam Harris twisted round to see what was happening, and now there was so much noise that he didn't have to be too careful.

Gawd, what a prospect. Lucky for him he hadn't got down there. Roasted or plugged. Not much of a choice. He could see Pastranou when the smoke cleared. Suppose that crazy bastard set the whole hill on fire? Sam began to shake all over again. If he ever got back to London it would be a hell of a long time before he tried foreign travel again, with or without a dolly bird.

Sam did some vigorous scratching. It was hot and airless under that bush, and Sam wasn't the only living thing there. When Pastranou started looking his way Sam's insides turned right over – where the hell could he hope to run to now? Up that bleeding slope? He'd never make it. He was no antelope.

When he realised that Pastranou wasn't really looking up at the bush but at something beyond it, Sam could have wept with a short relief. And he saw Ellen making her way down to the fire.

When she reached Pastranou she said harshly, 'Now who's the fool? You'll rouse the whole countryside with that – he's not in there, can't you see he isn't?'

Pastranou said nothing.

'Listen to me,' said Ellen urgently. 'It's all downhill, he's miles away down in the valley by now, he must be ... you've lost him, Peter...'

Slowly he turned his head to look at her. 'And whose fault is that? You think I arrange all this for a fool like you to spoil?'

'I'm not going to say I'm sorry,' she said. 'I couldn't just watch you shoot him–'

'George will be delighted to hear it,' he said.

'He's gone,' she said. 'He's probably down in that wood by now, Peter, you must listen to me – it won't spoil things for us, he doesn't understand a word of Italian, he doesn't know where he is now, he's lost and he's frightened ... so even if he does meet somebody they'll never know what he's talking about – it will still give us time.'

'It is untidy,' said Pastranou, gazing down the hillside to where the wood began in the valley. 'If I had the men and the time I would get him out of there, I would give him good reason to be frightened.'

'You're still sorry you didn't kill him,' she said.

'And you are a stupid and interfering woman,' he told her.

'It doesn't matter now,' she said. 'He got away and I'm glad.'

'This is enemy country for me as well as

for George,' he said. 'I would not wish to be here unless I had work to do, so you will not expect me to share your joy – I would shoot a dozen men like Harris to make sure of myself and George.'

Most of the bushes had almost burnt themselves out; patches of grass had caught, little tendrils of flame running out until they died when they reached the rocks and the shale. There were black twisted branches, stripped of their foliage. Grey flakes floated in the breeze. A small area of desolation, some of it still smouldering.

'We'd better go now,' said Ellen.

'I have never been concerned in something so stupid and clumsy. It offends me.' Peter Pastranou started back up the slope, and Ellen came after him.

Sam watched them go out of sight, and he wasn't going to move himself for a long long time. He wasn't going back near that car. They had the grub and he suspected he wasn't going to eat much that day, but that crazy bloke with the gun would be sitting up there just waiting for Sam to pop up and get his head blown off. From where he was hiding he'd never hear the car move off.

So don't push your luck any further,

Sammie boy. Sweat it out. Anything was better than a bullet in the noggin.

He could do with a drink and a smoke and he couldn't have either. That was as close as he had come to a sudden exit, and all for nothing – it didn't make any sense, and nobody who knew him would ever believe it happened that way.

One minute the bloke had been as nice and friendly as anybody could wish, and the next minute he was pumping slugs at you and setting fire to the country. Add that one up. There wasn't any reason to it.

When he felt it was reasonably safe he crawled out from the bush. His watch had been smashed when he did his dive down the slope, and he had no idea of the time – it must be early afternoon. He scuttled down past the scene of the fire – it might well have been his grave, and the thought gave him extra speed. Nobody shot at him and he didn't spend any time looking back.

As agile as any gazelle, he nipped down to that thick sheltering wood. Very soon he was hopelessly lost and he didn't give a damn. It was shady and dim, and if he kept on walking he'd get somewhere in the end.

It would take more than some treacherous git with a gun to fix Sam Harris.

11

Peter Pastranou drove in silence, Ellen sitting beside him like a dummy, gazing straight ahead and seeing nothing of the country they were passing through. The sun was hot and there was no shade on the hill road, and little cooling air came in through the car's open windows.

In spite of the incident with Sam Harris they reached the rendezvous with time to spare, and Pastranou pulled on to the grass edge, where the Ford Escort would be readily visible to Daniele and George, who should soon be approaching it from the crest of the hills behind them.

Pastranou got out the picnic basket. Ellen would eat nothing, even refusing coffee.

'You punish yourself because you think I am no more than a bloodthirsty bandit,' said Pastranou. 'It does me no harm.'

He chewed on cheese rolls, poured himself some coffee, and smiled at her unbending profile.

'You should not be so angry,' he said

mildly. 'The man escaped. You may have cause to regret your intrusion, we are still in enemy country – he knows you, he knows the car, and he knows me.'

She gave him no answer.

'We have no room for sentiment, Ellen. It is a weakness we cannot afford now – sentiment muddles the mind.'

She folded her hands in her lap. 'My mind is clear enough,' she said stiffly. 'It would have been cold-blooded murder; you weren't going to give him a chance.'

'Fair play,' said Pastranou mockingly. 'How cosy, and how stupid ... of what importance is a man like that? Measured against George Missounis? Come, my dear, your mind is full of nonsense, emotional nonsense.'

Abruptly she got out of the car, walked over to the only piece of shade under a bush, and sat with her back to him. Pastranou laughed and he went on with his meagre lunch. She had never heard the full story of what had happened near Genoa. One day, and soon perhaps, he would get George to tell her, then she might begin to know the real price of being hunted by the police.

It was mid-afternoon when Daniele came over the crest, with George limping behind him – a very bedraggled and unshaven George who had found the last five miles up and down the hills rather more than he could easily manage.

Ellen met them at the bottom and though she wouldn't have known him, until he smiled and said, 'A sight for sore eyes. Have you got an English cigarette and a drink?'

Pastranou was holding up the picnic basket when there was the sound of a small popping engine, and a Lambretta appeared down the road.

Dino was not in uniform, because strictly he was not on duty; he was taking a short cut to visit an aunt from whom he had modest expectations.

He braked and stopped and smiled as he wished the party *Buon giorno* all round. English tourists evidently, from their car. The Signorina smiled back at him, a little nervously he thought, and said it was a lovely day. The three men had poor manners – one of them actually turned his back, and the older one with the basket just nodded and put his head inside the car.

Dino wished them a pleasant journey, and got the Lambretta going again, and he was puzzled to think they were so plainly glad to see him move off. He was used to that kind of unfriendly reaction from the village locals, but English tourists couldn't know he was from the police.

Dino drove a little way down the road and stopped to give the matter some thought. That one who had turned his back, just as though he didn't want his face to be seen, Dino began to have an idea he had seen him before. He hadn't been dressed like the kind of tourist who would be in a car – and there was the other one with the girl as well, looking like a tramp.

Two rough looking men. A girl and an older man who looked respectable. That made a strange party to meet up there in the hills.

Dino had a good memory, he thought. A good policeman had to cultivate his memory. As he straddled the Lambretta Dino was linking Maddalena's place at San Bartolomeo with the man who had turned his back. So Aunt Francesca would have to wait a while for her favourite nephew.

'That was the copper from San Bartolomeo,' said Daniele. 'I know the louse well enough–'

'Does he know you?' said Pastranou quickly.

'I've seen him in Maddalena's place,' said Daniele. 'He probably saw me. Maybe he didn't recognise me—'

'And maybe he did,' said Pastranou abruptly.

'He's nosy that one,' said Daniele. 'So you'd better shift while you got the time.'

Pastranou took an envelope out of his pocket. This was Daniele's pay-off. He also gave him the keys of the Fiat he had left in a garage in San Remo. 'Whatever you get for it is yours, Daniele. A bonus. Is Angelo all right?'

Daniele nodded. 'He'll get his cut, when I see him.'

George Missounis was drinking coffee and listening. 'If that nark turns up again we should be able to manage him, three of us, so what's the panic?'

'I got all my fingers crossed,' said Daniele. 'Listen – he's coming...' Daniele darted across the road and plunged down the hill-side.

'Come on, George,' shouted Pastranou, getting into the car where Ellen already sat in the back.

Dino reappeared in time to see George

Missounis running to the car and noted the distinct limp. One man had vanished. The car turned dangerously in the narrow space and Dino almost rammed his Lambretta into its back, and he had an excellent view of the frightened face of the girl in the rear window. On a good road he knew he could never hope to keep up with the car, but he knew every bump and rut on this hilly track, all the sharp turns and twisting rises and the treacherous pieces of the surface, where it was doubly dangerous to brake too suddenly, even with four wheels.

He kept in touch. The Lambretta bounced and hummed and jigged about, and he cut the many corners closer than any car could.

He knew all the routes they could be heading for. Ever since the fiasco at the *Casa dei Vento* extra police checks had been set up. If he could reach a telephone in time … if he could stay with them long enough and if they didn't turn off and steer up into the hills where he might lose them again … they were some fifty yards in front but easy to follow because of the dust they were raising, and when they branched off he followed and was able to narrow the gap because they had unwisely chosen an even worse road.

And along here Dino was remembering there was a farmer with a telephone. So he let them get further ahead and looked for the lane leading to the farm. The credit would be his, even if somebody else stopped them.

'I – I can't see him,' said Ellen, peering back. 'I think we've lost him...'

She was being tossed about in the back of the car, and most of the time she had to shut her eyes when they seemed to be heading straight into disaster.

Peter Pastranou pointed to the line of telegraph poles slanting across the hill. 'Phone,' he shouted. 'First one we've seen ... wish to hell I knew where we are. If we can get a bit nearer the frontier we'll ditch the car ... I can take us across into France.'

'Make for a town and scatter,' said Missounis. 'Too many of us. Could we make Turin?'

Pastranou hunched his shoulders, and went on driving. They wouldn't reach Turin without being stopped, and the Lambretta didn't reappear. There was just an outside chance, if they got far enough west quickly enough, and that meant finding a better road, if there was one, and not a main road at that because all the main roads would be patrolled.

Forty minutes later they were in fact making good time on a road with a better surface and not so many of those dangerous tight bends that came up so suddenly. There were farm buildings stuck among the trees here and there – and telephone lines; fields under cultivation; they overtook a crowded country autobus, they began to meet other cars; there were occasional signposts but they met them too quickly to read them.

All the time they were heading west, which was what Pastranou wanted. The further west they got the better. He had been in worse spots and he was not unduly alarmed. Another ten or fifteen miles and they would abandon the car at some suitable place, and continue on foot. He would take them over the frontier.

It was ironic to think that one stupid country policeman on a scooter had messed it all and made it untidy. So they would have to improvise.

He told the other two how it was going to be. Ellen said nothing, she was too scared even to hear him. George wanted to argue. He thought Pastranou was exaggerating their position. Nothing had happened yet, and it was nearly an hour since they had lost the copper on his damned scooter.

Sam Harris went on walking and walking. He had blisters on both heels and a raging thirst and a conviction that he was completely lost. They'd find his shrivelled corpse in the bushes and they would never know who he was or why he had met his end. What a lousy way to finish up.

He had lost his passport, probably when he had been bouncing down that flaming hill with the bullets buzzing around him. He had his wallet with some cash, and a few cigarettes, but they didn't help his thirst much.

Maybe he was going round in circles, that's what happened to blokes lost in the jungle and this was as bad as any jungle. Under the trees he couldn't even spot the sky most of them, and all the bleeding trees looked the same.

He found a place where some water trickled over some green rocks, and he tried it. It was wet and it tasted of rusty nails.

He met a strange gink who was looking after some shaggy goats in a clearing, but they didn't have much of a conversation, not even after Sam had given him one of his few cigarettes.

Sam said 'San Remo' very distinctly several times and pointed here and there, and the dumb bloke grinned and nodded and didn't know what the hell he was on about.

He held out his hand for another cigarette, and Sam told him to get knotted in good plain English, and voyaged on. The goat merchant shouted something after him that didn't sound like any polite direction at all.

He got himself liberated from all those trees at last. He climbed some hills that really creased him, but he didn't feel quite so lost because he could see the sky. All the same, there wasn't much bounce left in him. He took plenty of rests, but he didn't dare take off his shoes because he'd never get them on again, and those blisters were giving him hell.

He couldn't believe it when he came up on a road. Not much of a road, more like a cart track. But it had to lead somewhere, even in this blasted deserted country. No cigarette. Nothing to drink, not even rusty nails. And that sun bashing down at him. Gawd.

He trudged along for half an hour or so,

221

growing more ragged and cheesed-off – and angry now at his lousy luck. Hiking wasn't Sam's thing. Somebody had been taking him for a mug. Ellen maybe. And that crazy bloke with a gun.

He overtook an old bloke perched up on a two-wheeled cart with a tired old horse and a load of sacked stuff in the back.

'San Remo?' said Sam hopefully.

The old boy grinned and beckoned him up. A friendly old coot. So Sam joined him on the plank that served as a seat. Anything was better than pounding his weary feet. They were making all of four miles an hour. The cart creaked and swayed and jolted, and the nice old boy was giving out with a lot of stuff that meant nothing to Sam, but he fancied he heard the name 'San Remo' here and there, so he did some nodding himself and they were all mates together.

After a while the old boy was snoozing, but the horse knew the way, it even seemed to have put on a little extra speed, so Sam guessed it might be heading for home and grub.

They came down a short hill, and there was a village. The driver woke and grinned at Sam and pointed to where a small dusty bus stood, and this time Sam was sure he was saying 'San Remo'.

When Sam pulled out his wallet, the old boy frowned and shook his head, and pointed at the bus.

Sam shook him warmly by the hand. 'Thanks a lot – you're the only friendly bloke I've met in this goddam place, and that's a fact. You're a beautiful old gent – okay?'

The old gent grinned. Perhaps he understood enough, and he wasn't insulted any more.

Sam limped across the square and climbed aboard the bus. There were a few passengers, most of them somnolent. There was one chick who looked okay, so Sam took a seat across from her and felt better already. Nice legs and a handy pair of Bristols. She didn't take any notice of him, and he couldn't blame her, because he looked like a proper tramp.

When the driver arrived and decided he might start, Sam held out a little bundle of lire notes and said 'San Remo' and got more change than he had expected. It was a country service, stopping everywhere, and it was early evening before he thought he began to recognise the outskirts of what must be the town. There was the cable railway he remembered, and the luxury villas; gardens and cars, and people. Civilisation at last.

He had to wander about a bit before he got on the road to the *Villa Rivarola,* and he was wondering just what he was going to find there: if Ellen was there with that Peter character there was going to be one hell of a sorting out, and nobody would be popping off at him with any guns, not this time. They wouldn't dare.

And if that was their idea of a joke then Sam Harris would put them both straight, and he was ready to say his piece good and strong in front of a flock of coppers, before he got the next plane home. The bastards.

The Ford Escort wasn't in the drive, but a snappy red Porsche was, and Kitty Dobell, in tight cream shorts and a blue spotted jersey, watched his dramatic arrival with interest.

'Hell,' she said, 'and what happened to you?'

'Somebody tried to liquidate me,' said Sam bitterly, limping over to the nearest chair.

'You're joking,' said Kitty. 'Aren't you?

Where's Ellen?'

'I wish I knew.' Very painfully Sam began to ease his shoes off. 'I have been chased up and down the bleeding mountains, that's what happened to me.'

'You poor thing,' said Kitty, smiling. 'Who did all that?'

'A bloke with Ellen,' said Sam. 'Have you seen them?'

'Not a sign,' said Kitty. 'I've only been here a few hours. You're not making much sense, Sam. I'll get you a drink and you can tell all – brandy all right?'

Sam was blowing tenderly on one of his blistered heels. 'Sooner do a beer – I didn't know you were coming.'

'Nice to see me?' said Kitty, increasing the radiance of her smile and standing in front of him so that he had to see it all.

'Very nice,' said Sam, giving her his wolf-ish grin slap between those cunning little breasts.

'I feared I might be intruding,' she said. 'Love-nest and all that jazz.'

'In a pig's eye,' said Sam. 'It's been a shambles all through.'

'It was just an idea I had,' said Kitty. 'I thought I'd like to see how you were making out.'

'No score at all,' said Sam, and he knew they were both talking of the same thing.

She brought him a long iced lager. 'Now you start at the beginning,' she said. 'I want to hear all of it.'

'In another few minutes I think we'd better start walking,' said Pastranou. 'I think we're clear now.'

Nobody said anything. Then they came round a corner, and there was the barrier in front, less than a hundred yards distant – the striped wooden bar closing most of the road, the police cars parked beside, men in uniform, some with guns in the sunshine. All now looking their way. One uniformed officer was walking towards them with both hands lifted.

Peter Pastranou hesitated.

'Go through, man! You can't stop now – it's our only chance!' George Missounis had hunched his shoulders, already bracing himself.

'No! No!' Ellen had scrambled forward. She was trying to get at Pastranou's hands on the wheel. She sobbed, slapping at his shoulders helplessly.

George Missounis leaned back and hit her across the face and said something that nobody else heard. Pastranou accelerated, hard and sharp. The leading officer in the road ran for the ditch and made it with no dignity.

There was a splintering of timber and glass as the car hit the barrier. It slewed sideways, swiped one of the parked cars. It was almost through, almost clear.

But the impact had slowed it down, and Pastranou was fighting to get it straight and into a lower gear, trying all the time to see through a shattered windscreen.

A policeman with a sub-machine gun, standing back from the barrier, had kept his head and opened up, aiming at the tyres, but his gun had jumped and he was off target. But he punched a line of bullet holes along the side of the car and then had time to repeat the treatment. The Ford swerved violently, swung across the road and dived through the hedge. It fell out of sight in the field below.

There followed some shouting and waving of arms, then a cautious approach to the gap in the hedge on the part of the men with guns.

The car lay on its side in the grass. Pastranou was heaving himself out of the door and he took no notice of their shouted commands to halt. He had his gun and he fired at the hedge and there was a concerted bobbing down of heads. He began to run across the grass to a belt of trees some fifty yards away, stumbling now and then, bending, weaving, but running, always running.

They lost sight of him in a dip in the ground, and those with weapons went in after him, spreading out and firing in concentrated bursts that covered all the area where he should have been.

But Peter Pastranou was elsewhere, crawling along the dip out of sight until he was within reach of the trees. With a sudden burst of speed he got in among the trees while bullets clipped bark from the trunks all around him. Then he was gone in the shade.

The officer in charge of the operation began to use his head at last. One of the policemen who was reckoned to be a marksman well above average was sent off in a car to post himself on the side road that ran at the back of the wood; there was a ditch and a wall there as well.

The wood was thin and they would drive the fugitive through, and the marksman would pick him off as he broke cover.

Pastranou lay on his belly, his revolver was now empty, and he knew he had some broken ribs when the car crashed. He also knew that George and Ellen were dead – he had been splashed with their blood when the machine gun got them just before they went through the hedge. He lay motionless for some minutes, listening, trying not to breathe too deeply because each breath was an agony.

He could hear them behind him, voices … they were nervous of course, even though there were so many of them. They would remember their meeting with Peter Pastranou. By God they would.

He had no idea of the extent of the wood. He could have waited by the car and let them take him, with the two dead bodies. But that would have been ignominious. Surrender was not in his creed. He began to crawl away from their questing voices, very painfully and very slowly – but he was moving, he was making the last defiant gesture, and the blood on his face was not yet his. He thought briefly of Joe Feeny and how right he had been proved – this was the last one, the one he was going to lose.

There was a scattering of shots behind him and some shouting, but not near, moving away. If the wood was thick enough, and if they didn't bring dogs in, if he could keep them guessing until dark – he could still give them a run for their money.

His breathing had become noisy and he couldn't stop himself grunting. He pulled himself upright, and saw that the trees were thinning and there was light ahead and glimpses of sky. He wiped the drying blood from his face and forced himself to go on, and now he was not seeing too clearly. When he was young this would have been nothing … it was the ageing body that beat a man first when the gods had him cornered to make sport of him. Gods or God?

Peter Pastranou reached the old grey wall with the moss and lichen and the crumbled mortar. He was pulling himself up to take a look and he looked the wrong way first. There was just one shot and the marksman put a bullet through his head.

When they came to take the shattered bodies from the wreck of the car, the Signorina aroused some pity because she had been so beautiful and so young, but then she had been in very bad company.

They found a British passport, made out to one Samuel Harris, with a London address, and the ranking officer present declared that it would certainly prove to be a forgery. It was added to the other exhibits.

Sam Harris had spent a pleasant and relaxing evening after his perilous experience in the open air. His blisters had been attended to by Kitty herself. He had bathed and changed into more snappy gear, and his outlook had improved beyond measure as the evening wore on.

There had been a dinner that he could tackle with relish, no foreign rubbish this time – steak, mushrooms, chips even, treacle tart no less, and booze. And Anna had wished them both a meaningful *buona notte* before she took herself off the premises.

Kitty had been interested in Sam's dramatic recital, and he had rehearsed just what he would say to those two when they showed up, and with each telling it became more effective and devastating. Nobody was going to take pot shots at Sam Harris and get away with it.

'They made a mug out of me,' he repeated irately, 'and that's what I don't get – why me? It was her idea to come here in the first place, and if that mad git wanted some target practice why pick on me? I only met him last night–'

'Peter something-or-other,' said Kitty. 'We don't know him, Sammie.'

'Big friend of your family, that's what I understood. Ellen knew him all right.'

'She was always a bit of a mystery,' said Kitty.

'She had me fooled,' said Sam. 'This looks like a put-up job, and I don't see any sense to it.'

'It couldn't have been some kind of a crazy way-out practical joke?' said Kitty.

'It didn't make me laugh much,' said Sam.

They were sitting side by side on a deep divan. Kitty stroked the back of his neck. She was being very attentive, and she really was a knock-out seen close to, and Sam's sense of grievance began to lose some of its sharpness.

A dolly-bird with money behind her, and on his side for a change – unless he mistook all the signs.

'I don't think they'll come here tonight now,' said Kitty. 'Whatever they've been up to, it would be a bit risky and they don't know what happened to you.'

'A pair of cheeky bastards,' said Sam. 'First thing tomorrow morning I'll nip round to the local police and give it to them, let them sort it out. And what am I gonna do about my passport? They won't let me out without it, will they? And I don't reckon on staying here much longer–'

Kitty smiled at his flushed face, and trailed one finger down the nape of his neck. 'Would that be such an awful hardship, Sammie?'

'Well that depends,' said Sam cautiously. 'I mean, it's been a lousy trip so far–'

'It might improve,' she said. 'You needn't worry about the passport; we'll see the consul as well as the police, he'll fix you up.'

'It was a funny business, right from the start,' said Sam. 'It beats me.'

She stood up and walking slowly went up the stairs. Sam watched her for a bit and told himself there was nothing to be nervous about. Also the whisky helped. He went up.

She was standing by the door of her room. 'Well, Sammie,' she said, 'are you all that tired?'

'Never felt better,' he said.

'Let's see about that, shall we?' She opened the door and he followed her in.

Thus it was that the *Villa Rivarola* witnessed some activities in tune with its earlier history, Kitty being an inventive and energetic partner, and far more experienced than Sam thought she had any right to be for her age. He didn't get much sleep. Sam's bonus.

In the morning the shooting at the road-block had become local news, and Sam's own part in the exploit had assumed heroic proportions, which Kitty found a bit of a giggle because by then she knew Sam pretty well, and whatever he was he was no hero.

His passport had been returned, and he had been interviewed by the press in the unlikely role of an upholder of the forces of Law and Order, which would have amused some of his associates back in London.

After four exhausting days and nights, Kitty decided she'd had enough of the hero, and invited him to move on. He was beginning to bore her – he was now wanting to sleep at night, imagine that for an insult. Also she had met up with a swinging crowd from a yacht in the harbour, rather more her style, including at least three males for whom she had some plans of a private nature which wouldn't need Sam's presence.

They could stuff their *Riviera dei Fiori,* and the *Villa Rivarola.* Sam went back by air, and he had to pay his own way, which took a bit of the shine off the bonus.

The next time a dolly bird offered him something for free, he would look at it twice, and run like hell the other way.

The publishers hope that this book has given you enjoyable reading. Large Print Books are especially designed to be as easy to see and hold as possible. If you wish a complete list of our books please ask at your local library or write directly to:

Dales Large Print Books
Magna House, Long Preston,
Skipton, North Yorkshire.
BD23 4ND